Christmas Stories

For Children

25 Stories and Verses

to Read Aloud

CONTENTS

FORWARD - Keeping Christmas

    Henry van Dyke   7

CHRISTMAS STORIES

Louisa May Alcott

    Tilly's Christmas   9

F. Arnstein

    Christmas in the Barn   17

Hans Christian Andersen

    The Little Match Girl   21

    The Fir Tree   25

    The Snow Man   36

Frank L. Baum

    A Kidnapped Santa Claus   43

    Little Bun Rabbit   57

Elizabeth Harrison

    Little Gretchen and the Wooden Shoe   65

Lewis Carroll

    Christmas Greetings from a Fairy to a Child   76

J. Stirling Coyne

    The Christmas Fairy of Strasburg:
    A German Folk-Tale   77

Charles Dickens

    The Cratchits' Christmas Dinner (Adapted)   81

    Christmas at Fezziwig's Warehouse   91

O. Henry

    The Gift of the Magi   94

Henry Wadsworth Longfellow

    I Heard the Bells On Christmas Day   102

Clement Clarke Moore

    'Twas the Night Before Christmas   104

John Strange Winter

    A Christmas Fairy   107

Harriet Beecher Stowe

    Christmas; or, The Good Fairy   112

The Brothers Grimm

    The Elves and the Shoemaker — 124

Leo Tolstoy

    Papa Panov's Special Christmas — 127

Anne Hollingsworth Wharton

    Christmas in Seventeen Seventy-Six — 133

Nora Smith

    Little Piccola — 140

Carolyn S. Bailey

    The Legend of Babouscka (Adapted) — 146

Winnifred E. Lincoln

    Little Girl's Christmas — 148

Florence M. Kingsley

    The Star — 156

Raymond McAlden

    Why the Chimes Rang — 161

FORWARD - KEEPING CHRISTMAS

By Henry van Dyke

ROMANS, xiv, 6: He that regardeth the day, regardeth it unto the Lord.

It is a good thing to observe Christmas day. The mere marking of times and seasons, when men agree to stop work and make merry together, is a wise and wholesome custom. It helps one to feel the supremacy of the common life over the individual life. It reminds a man to set his own little watch, now and then, by the great clock of humanity which runs on sun time.

But there is a better thing than the observance of Christmas day, and that is, keeping Christmas.

Are you willing to forget what you have done for other people, and to remember what other people have done for you; to ignore what the world owes you, and to think what you owe the world; to put your rights in the background, and your duties in the middle distance, and your chances to do a little more than your duty in the foreground; to see that your fellow-men are just as real as you are, and try to look behind their faces to their hearts, hungry for joy; to own that probably the only good reason for your existence is not what you are going to get out of life, but what you are going to give to life; to close your book of complaints against the management of the universe, and look around you for a place where you can sow a few seeds of happiness--are you willing to do these things even for a day? Then you can keep Christmas.

Are you willing to stoop down and consider the needs and the desires of little children; to remember the weakness and loneliness of people who are growing old; to stop asking how much your friends love you, and ask yourself whether you love them enough; to bear in mind the things that other people have to bear on their hearts; to try to understand what those who live in the same house with you really want, without waiting for them to tell you; to trim your lamp so that it will give more light and less smoke, and to carry it in front so that your shadow will fall behind you; to make a grave for your ugly thoughts, and a garden for your kindly feelings, with the gate open--are you willing to do these things even for a day? Then you can keep Christmas.

Are you willing to believe that love is the strongest thing in the world--stronger than hate, stronger than evil, stronger than death--and that the blessed life which began in Bethlehem nineteen hundred years ago is the image and brightness of the Eternal Love? Then you can keep Christmas.

And if you keep it for a day, why not always?

But you can never keep it alone.

TILLY'S CHRISTMAS

By Louisa May Alcott

"I'm so glad to-morrow is Christmas, because I'm going to have lots of presents."

"So am I glad, though I don't expect any presents but a pair of mittens."

"And so am I; but I shan't have any presents at all."

As the three little girls trudged home from school they said these things, and as Tilly spoke, both the others looked at her with pity and some surprise, for she spoke cheerfully, and they wondered how she could be happy when she was so poor she could have no presents on Christmas.

"Don't you wish you could find a purse full of money right here in the path?" said Kate, the child who was going to have "lots of presents."

"Oh, don't I, if I could keep it honestly!" and Tilly's eyes shone at the very thought.

"What would you buy?" asked Bessy, rubbing her cold hands, and longing for her mittens.

"I'd buy a pair of large, warm blankets, a load of wood, a shawl for mother, and a pair of shoes for me; and if there was enough left, I'd give Bessy a new hat, and then she needn't wear Ben's old felt one," answered Tilly.

The girls laughed at that ; but Bessy pulled the funny hat over her ears, and said she was much obliged, but she'd rather have candy.

"Let's look, and may be we can find a purse. People are always going about with money at Christmas time, and some one may lose it here," said Kate.

So, as they went along the snowy road, they looked about them, half in earnest, half in fun. Suddenly Tilly sprang forward, exclaiming,

"I see it! I've found it!"

The others followed, but all stopped disappointed; for it wasn't a purse, it was only a little bird. It lay upon the snow with its wings spread and feebly fluttering, as if too weak to fly. Its little feet were benumbed with cold; its once bright eyes were dull with pain, and instead of a blithe song, it could only utter a faint chirp, now and then, as if crying for help.

"Nothing but a stupid old robin; how provoking!" cried Kate, sitting down to rest.

"I shan't touch it. I found one once, and took care of it, and the ungrateful thing flew away the minute it was well," said Bessy, creeping under Kate's shawl, and putting her hands under her chin to warm them.

"Poor little birdie! How pitiful he looks, and how glad he must be to see some one coming to help him! I'll take him up gently, and carry him home to mother. Don't be frightened, dear, I'm your friend;" and Tilly knelt down in the snow, stretching her hand to the bird with the tenderest pity in her face.

Kate and Bessy laughed.

"Don't stop for that thing; it's getting late and cold: let's go on and look for the purse," they said, moving away.

"You wouldn't leave it to die?' cried Tilly.

"I'd rather have the bird than the money, so I shan't look any more. The purse wouldn't be mine, and I should only be tempted to keep it; but this poor thing will thank and love me, and I'm so glad I came in time."

Gently lifting the bird, Tilly felt its tiny cold claws cling to her hand, and saw its dim eyes brighten as it nestled down with a grateful chirp.

"Now I've got a Christmas present after all," she said, smiling, as -they walked on. " I always wanted a bird, and this one will be such a pretty pet for me!"

"He'll fly away the first chance he gets, and die anyhow; so you'd better not waste your time over him," said Bessy.

"He can't pay you for taking care of him, and my mother says it isn't worth while to help folks that can't help us," added Kate.

"My mother says, 'Do as you'd be done by;' and I'm sure I'd like any one to help me if I was dying of cold and hunger.' Love your neighbor as yourself? is another of her sayings. This bird is my little neighbor, and I'll love him and care for him, as I often wish our rich neighbor would love and care for us," answered Tilly, breathing her warm breath over the benumbed bird, who looked up at her with confiding eyes, quick to feel and know a friend.

"What a funny girl you are," said Kate; "caring for that silly bird, and talking about loving your neighbor in that sober way. Mr. King don't care a bit for you, and never will, though he knows how poor you are; so I don't think your plan amounts to much."

"I believe it, though; and shall do my part, any way. Good-night. I hope you'll have a merry Christmas, and lots of pretty things," answered Tilly, as they parted.

Her eyes were full, and she felt so poor as she went on alone toward the little old house where she lived. It would have been so pleasant to know that she was going to have some of the pretty things all children love to find in their full stockings on Christmas morning. And pleasanter still to have been able to give her mother something nice. So many comforts were needed, and there was no hope of getting them; for they could barely get food and fire.

"Never mind, birdie, we'll make the best of what we have, and be merry in spite of every thing. You shall have a happy Christmas, any way; and I know God won't forget us, if every one else does."

She stopped a minute to wipe her eyes, and lean her cheek against the bird's soft breast, finding great comfort in the little creature, though it could only love her, nothing more.

"See, mother, what a nice present I've found," she cried, going in with a cheery face that was like sunshine in the dark room.

"I'm glad of that, dearie; for I haven't been able to get my little girl any thing but a rosy apple. Poor bird! Give it some of your warm bread and milk."

"Why, mother, what a big bowlful ! I'm afraid you gave me all the milk," said Tilly, smiling over the nice, steaming supper that stood ready for her.

"I've had plenty, dear. Sit down and dry your wet feet, and put the bird in my basket on this warm flannel."

Tilly peeped into the closet and saw nothing there but dry bread.

"Mother's given me all the milk, and is going without her tea, 'cause she knows I'm hungry. Now I'll surprise her, and she shall have a good supper too. She is going to split wood, and I'll fix it while she's gone."

So Tilly put down the old tea-pot, carefully poured out a part of the milk, and from her pocket produced a great, plummy bun, that one of the school-children had given her, and she had saved for her mother. A slice of the dry bread was nicely toasted, and the bit of butter set by for her put on it. When her mother came in there was the table drawn up in a warm place, a hot cup of tea ready, and Tilly and birdie waiting for her.

Such a poor little supper, and yet such a happy one; for love, charity, and contentment were guests there, and that Christmas eve was a blither one than that up at the great house, where lights shone, fires blazed, a great tree glittered, and music sounded, as the children danced and played.

"We must go to bed early, for we've only wood enough to last over to-morrow. I shall be paid for my work the day after, and then we can get some," said Tilly's mother, as they sat by the fire.

"If my bird was only a fairy bird, and would give us three wishes, how nice it would be! Poor dear, he can't give me any thing; but it's no matter," answered Tilly, looking at the robin, who lay in the basket with his head under his wing, a mere little feathery bunch.

"He can give you one thing, Tilly, the pleasure of doing good. That is one of the sweetest things in life; and the poor can enjoy it as well as the rich."

As her mother spoke, with her tired hand softly stroking her little daughter's hair, Tilly suddenly started and pointed to the window, saying, in a frightened whisper,

"I saw a face, a man's face, looking in! It's gone now; but I truly saw it."

"Some traveller attracted by the light perhaps. I'll go and see." And Tilly's mother went to the door.

No one was there. The wind blew cold, the stars shone, the snow lay white on field and wood, and the Christmas moon was glittering in the sky.

"What sort of a face was it?" asked Tilly's mother, coming back.

"A pleasant sort of face, I think; but I was so startled I don't quite know what it was like. I wish we had a curtain there," said Tilly.

"I like to have our light shine out in the evening, for the road is dark and lonely just here, and the twinkle of our lamp is pleasant to people's eyes as they go by. We can do so little for our neighbors, I am glad to cheer the way for them. Now put these poor old shoes to dry, and go to bed, dearie; I'll come soon."

Tilly went, taking her bird with her to sleep in his basket near by, lest he should be lonely in the night.

Soon the little house was dark and still, and no one saw the Christmas spirits at their work that night.

When Tilly opened the door next morning, she gave a loud cry, clapped her hands, and then stood still, quite speechless with wonder and delight. There, before the door, lay a great pile of wood, all ready to burn, a big bundle and a basket; with a lovely nosegay of winter roses, holly, and evergreen tied to the handle.

"Oh, mother! did the fairies do it?" cried Tilly, pale with her happiness, as she seized the basket, while her mother took in the bundle.

"Yes, dear, the best and dearest fairy in the world, called 'Charity.' She walks abroad at Christmas time, does beautiful deeds like this, and does not stay to be thanked," answered her mother with full eyes, as she undid the parcel.

There they were, the warm, thick blankets, the comfortable shawl, the new shoes, and, best of all, a pretty winter hat for Bessy. The basket was full of good things to eat, and on the flowers lay a paper saying,

"For the little girl who loves her neighbor as herself."

"Mother, I really think my bird is a fairy bird, and all these splendid things come from him," said Tilly, laughing and crying with joy.

It really did seem so, for as she spoke, the robin flew to the table, hopped to the nosegay, and perching among the roses, began to chirp with all his little might. The sun streamed in on flowers, bird, and happy child, and no one saw a shadow glide away from the window; no one ever knew that Mr. King had seen and heard the little girls the night before, or dreamed that the rich neighbor had learned a lesson from the poor neighbor.

And Tilly's bird was a fairy bird; for by her love and tenderness to the helpless thing, she brought good gifts to herself, happiness to the unknown giver of them, and a faithful little friend who did not fly away, but stayed with her till the snow was gone, making summer for her in the winter-time.

CHRISTMAS IN THE BARN

F. Arnstein

Only two more days and Christmas would be here! It had been snowing hard, and Johnny was standing at the window, looking at the soft, white snow which covered the ground half a foot deep. Presently he heard the noise of wheels coming up the road, and a wagon turned in at the gate and came past the window. Johnny was very curious to know what the wagon could be bringing. He pressed his little nose close to the cold window pane, and to his great surprise, saw two large Christmas-trees. Johnny wondered why there were TWO trees, and turned quickly to run and tell mamma all about it; but then remembered that mamma was not at home. She had gone to the city to buy some Christmas presents and would not return until quite late. Johnny began to feel that his toes and fingers had grown quite cold from standing at the window so long; so he drew his own little chair up to the cheerful grate fire and sat there quietly thinking. Pussy, who had been curled up like a little bundle of wool, in the very warmest corner, jumped up, and, going to Johnny, rubbed her head against his knee to attract his attention. He patted her gently and began to talk to her about what was in his thoughts.

He had been puzzling over the TWO trees which had come, and at last had made up his mind about them. "I know now, Pussy," said he, "why there are two trees. This morning when I kissed Papa good-bye at the gate he said he was going to buy one for me, and mamma, who was busy in the house, did not hear him say so; and I am sure she must have bought the other. But what shall we do with two Christmas-trees?"

Pussy jumped into his lap and purred and purred. A plan suddenly flashed into Johnny's mind. "Would you like to have one, Pussy?" Pussy purred more loudly, and it seemed almost as though she had said yes.

"Oh! I will, I will! if mamma will let me. I'll have a Christmas-tree out in the bam for you, Pussy, and for all the pets; and then you'll all be as happy as I shall be with my tree in the parlour."

By this time it had grown quite late. There was a ring at the door-bell; and quick as a flash Johnny ran, with happy, smiling face, to meet papa and mamma and gave them each a loving kiss. During the evening he told them all that he had done that day and also about the two big trees which the man had brought. It was just as Johnny had thought. Papa and mamma had each bought one, and as it was so near Christmas they thought they would not send either of them back. Johnny was very glad of this, and told them of the happy plan he had made and asked if he might have the extra tree. Papa and mamma smiled a little as Johnny explained his plan but they said he might have the tree, and Johnny went to bed feeling very happy.

That night his papa fastened the tree into a block of wood so that it would stand firmly and then set it in the middle of the barn floor. The next day when Johnny had finished his lessons he went to the kitchen, and asked Annie, the cook, if she would save the bones and potato parings and all other leavings from the day's meals and give them to him the following morning. He also begged her to give him several cupfuls of salt and cornmeal, which she did, putting them in paper bags for him. Then she gave him the dishes he asked for—a few chipped ones not good enough to be used at table—and an old wooden bowl. Annie wanted to know what Johnny intended to do with all these things, but he only said: "Wait until to-morrow, then you shall see." He gathered up all the things which the cook had given him and carried them to the barn, placing them on a shelf in one corner, where he was sure no one would touch them and where they would be all ready for him to use the next morning.

Christmas morning came, and, as soon as he could, Johnny hurried out to the barn, where stood the Christmas-tree which he was going to trim for all his pets. The first thing he did was to get a paper bag of oats; this he tied to one of the branches of the tree, for Brownie the mare. Then he made up several bundles of hay and tied these on the other side of the tree, not quite so high up, where White Face, the cow, could reach them; and on the lowest branches some more hay for Spotty, the calf.

Next Johnny hurried to the kitchen to get the things Annie had promised to save for him. She had plenty to give. With his arms and hands full he went back to the barn. He found three "lovely" bones with plenty of meat on them; these he tied together to another branch of the tree, for Rover, his big black dog. Under the tree he placed the big wooden bowl, and filled it well with potato parings, rice, and meat, left from yesterday's dinner; this was the "full and tempting trough" for Piggywig. Near this he placed a bowl of milk for Pussy, on one plate the salt for the pet lamb, and on another the cornmeal for the dear little chickens. On the top of the tree he tied a basket of nuts; these were for his pet squirrel; and I had almost forgotten to tell you of the bunch of carrots tied very low down where soft white Bunny could reach them.

When all was done, Johnny stood off a little way to look at this wonderful Christmas-tree. Clapping his hands with delight, he ran to call papa and mamma and Annie, and they laughed aloud when they saw what he had done. It was the funniest Christmas-tree they had ever seen. They were sure the pets would like the presents Johnny had chosen.

Then there was a busy time in the barn. Papa and mamma and Annie helped about bringing in the animals, and before long, Brownie, White Face, Spotty, Rover, Piggywig, Pussy, Lambkin, the chickens, the squirrel and Bunny, the rabbit, had been led each to his own Christmas breakfast on and under the tree. What a funny sight it was to see them all standing around looking happy and contented, eating and drinking with such an appetite!

While watching them Johnny had another thought, and he ran quickly to the house, and brought out the new trumpet which papa had given him for Christmas. By this time the animals had all finished their breakfast and Johnny gave a little toot on his trumpet as a signal that the tree festival was over. Brownie went, neighing and prancing, to her stall, White Face walked demurely off with a bellow, which Spotty, the calf, running at her heels, tried to imitate; the little lamb skipped bleating away; Piggywig walked off with a grunt; Pussy jumped on the fence with a mew; the squirrel still sat up in the tree cracking her nuts; Bunny hopped to her snug little quarters; while Rover, barking loudly, chased the chickens back to their coop. Such a hubbub of noises! Mamma said it sounded as if they were trying to say "Merry Christmas to you, Johnny! Merry Christmas to all."

THE LITTLE MATCH GIRL

By Hans Christian Andersen

Most terribly cold it was; it snowed, and was nearly quite dark, and evening—the last evening of the year. In this cold and darkness there went along the street a poor little girl, bareheaded, and with naked feet. When she left home she had slippers on, it is true; but what was the good of that? They were very large slippers, which her mother had hitherto worn; so large were they; and the poor little thing lost them as she scuffled away across the street, because of two carriages that rolled by dreadfully fast.

One slipper was nowhere to be found; the other had been laid hold of by an urchin, and off he ran with it; he thought it would do capitally for a cradle when he some day or other should have children himself. So the little maiden walked on with her tiny naked feet, that were quite red and blue from cold. She carried a quantity of matches in an old apron, and she held a bundle of them in her hand. Nobody had bought anything of her the whole livelong day; no one had given her a single farthing.

She crept along trembling with cold and hunger—a very picture of sorrow, the poor little thing!

The flakes of snow covered her long fair hair, which fell in beautiful curls around her neck; but of that, of course, she never once now thought. From all the windows the candles were gleaming, and it smelt so deliciously of roast goose, for you know it was New Year's Eve; yes, of that she thought.

In a corner formed by two houses, of which one advanced more than the other, she seated herself down and cowered together. Her little feet she had drawn close up to her, but she grew colder and colder, and to go home she did not venture, for she had not sold any matches and could not bring a farthing of money: from her father she would certainly get blows, and at home it was cold too, for above her she had only the roof, through which the wind whistled, even though the largest cracks were stopped up with straw and rags.

Her little hands were almost numbed with cold. Oh! a match might afford her a world of comfort, if she only dared take a single one out of the bundle, draw it against the wall, and warm her fingers by it. She drew one out. "Rischt!" how it blazed, how it burnt! It was a warm, bright flame, like a candle, as she held her hands over it: it was a wonderful light. It seemed really to the little maiden as though she were sitting before a large iron stove, with burnished brass feet and a brass ornament at top. The fire burned with such blessed influence; it warmed so delightfully. The little girl had already stretched out her feet to warm them too; but—the small flame went out, the stove vanished: she had only the remains of the burnt-out match in her hand.

She rubbed another against the wall: it burned brightly, and where the light fell on the wall, there the wall became transparent like a veil, so that she could see into the room. On the table was spread a snow-white tablecloth; upon it was a splendid porcelain service, and the roast goose was steaming famously with its stuffing of apple and dried plums. And what was still more capital to behold was, the goose hopped down from the dish, reeled about on the floor with knife and fork in its breast, till it came up to the poor little girl; when—the match went out and nothing but the thick, cold, damp wall was left behind. She lighted another match. Now there she was sitting under the most magnificent Christmas tree: it was still larger, and more decorated than the one which she had seen through the glass door in the rich merchant's house.

Thousands of lights were burning on the green branches, and gaily-colored pictures, such as she had seen in the shop-windows, looked down upon her. The little maiden stretched out her hands towards them when—the match went out. The lights of the Christmas tree rose higher and higher, she saw them now as stars in heaven; one fell down and formed a long trail of fire.

"Someone is just dead!" said the little girl; for her old grandmother, the only person who had loved her, and who was now no more, had told her, that when a star falls, a soul ascends to God.

She drew another match against the wall: it was again light, and in the lustre there stood the old grandmother, so bright and radiant, so mild, and with such an expression of love.

"Grandmother!" cried the little one. "Oh, take me with you! You go away when the match burns out; you vanish like the warm stove, like the delicious roast goose, and like the magnificent Christmas tree!" And she rubbed the whole bundle of matches quickly against the wall, for she wanted to be quite sure of keeping her grandmother near her. And the matches gave such a brilliant light that it was brighter than at noon-day: never formerly had the grandmother been so beautiful and so tall. She took the little maiden, on her arm, and both flew in brightness and in joy so high, so very high, and then above was neither cold, nor hunger, nor anxiety—they were with God.

But in the corner, at the cold hour of dawn, sat the poor girl, with rosy cheeks and with a smiling mouth, leaning against the wall—frozen to death on the last evening of the old year. Stiff and stark sat the child there with her matches, of which one bundle had been burnt. "She wanted to warm herself," people said. No one had the slightest suspicion of what beautiful things she had seen; no one even dreamed of the splendor in which, with her grandmother she had entered on the joys of a new year.

THE FIR TREE

By Hans Christian Andersen

Out in the woods stood a nice little Fir Tree. The place he had was a very good one: the sun shone on him: as to fresh air, there was enough of that, and round him grew many large-sized comrades, pines as well as firs. But the little Fir wanted so very much to be a grown-up tree.

He did not think of the warm sun and of the fresh air; he did not care for the little cottage children that ran about and prattled when they were in the woods looking for wild-strawberries. The children often came with a whole pitcher full of berries, or a long row of them threaded on a straw, and sat down near the young tree and said, "Oh, how pretty he is! What a nice little fir!" But this was what the Tree could not bear to hear.

At the end of a year he had shot up a good deal, and after another year he was another long bit taller; for with fir trees one can always tell by the shoots how many years old they are.

"Oh! Were I but such a high tree as the others are," sighed he. "Then I should be able to spread out my branches, and with the tops to look into the wide world! Then would the birds build nests among my branches: and when there was a breeze, I could bend with as much stateliness as the others!"

Neither the sunbeams, nor the birds, nor the red clouds which morning and evening sailed above him, gave the little Tree any pleasure.

In winter, when the snow lay glittering on the ground, a hare would often come leaping along, and jump right over the little Tree. Oh, that made him so angry! But two winters were past, and in the third the Tree was so large that the hare was obliged to go round it. "To grow and grow, to get older and be tall," thought the Tree—"that, after all, is the most delightful thing in the world!"

In autumn the wood-cutters always came and felled some of the largest trees. This happened every year; and the young Fir Tree, that had now grown to a very comely size, trembled at the sight; for the magnificent great trees fell to the earth with noise and cracking, the branches were lopped off, and the trees looked long and bare; they were hardly to be recognised; and then they were laid in carts, and the horses dragged them out of the wood.

Where did they go to? What became of them?

In spring, when the swallows and the storks came, the Tree asked them, "Don't you know where they have been taken? Have you not met them anywhere?"

The swallows did not know anything about it; but the Stork looked musing, nodded his head, and said, "Yes; I think I know; I met many ships as I was flying hither from Egypt; on the ships were magnificent masts, and I venture to assert that it was they that smelt so of fir. I may congratulate you, for they lifted themselves on high most majestically!"

"Oh, were I but old enough to fly across the sea! But how does the sea look in reality? What is it like?"

"That would take a long time to explain," said the Stork, and with these words off he went.

"Rejoice in thy growth!" said the Sunbeams. "Rejoice in thy vigorous growth, and in the fresh life that moveth within thee!"

And the Wind kissed the Tree, and the Dew wept tears over him; but the Fir understood it not.

When Christmas came, quite young trees were cut down: trees which often were not even as large or of the same age as this Fir Tree, who could never rest, but always wanted to be off. These young trees, and they were always the finest looking, retained their branches; they were laid on carts, and the horses drew them out of the wood.

"Where are they going to?" asked the Fir. "They are not taller than I; there was one indeed that was considerably shorter; and why do they retain all their branches? Whither are they taken?"

"We know! We know!" chirped the Sparrows. "We have peeped in at the windows in the town below! We know whither they are taken! The greatest splendor and the greatest magnificence one can imagine await them. We peeped through the windows, and saw them planted in the middle of the warm room and ornamented with the most splendid things, with gilded apples, with gingerbread, with toys, and many hundred lights!"

"And then?" asked the Fir Tree, trembling in every bough. "And then? What happens then?"

"We did not see anything more: it was incomparably beautiful."

"I would fain know if I am destined for so glorious a career," cried the Tree, rejoicing. "That is still better than to cross the sea! What a longing do I suffer! Were Christmas but come! I am now tall, and my branches spread like the others that were carried off last year! Oh! were I but already on the cart! Were I in the warm room with all the splendor and magnificence! Yes; then something better, something still grander, will surely follow, or wherefore should they thus ornament me? Something better, something still grander must follow—but what? Oh, how I long, how I suffer! I do not know myself what is the matter with me!"

"Rejoice in our presence!" said the Air and the Sunlight. "Rejoice in thy own fresh youth!"

But the Tree did not rejoice at all; he grew and grew, and was green both winter and summer. People that saw him said, "What a fine tree!" and towards Christmas he was one of the first that was cut down. The axe struck deep into the very pith; the Tree fell to the earth with a sigh; he felt a pang—it was like a swoon; he could not think of happiness, for he was sorrowful at being separated from his home, from the place where he had sprung up. He well knew that he should never see his dear old comrades, the little bushes and flowers around him, anymore; perhaps not even the birds! The departure was not at all agreeable.

The Tree only came to himself when he was unloaded in a court-yard with the other trees, and heard a man say, "That one is splendid! We don't want the others." Then two servants came in rich livery and carried the Fir Tree into a large and splendid drawing-room. Portraits were hanging on the walls, and near the white porcelain stove stood two large Chinese vases with lions on the covers. There, too, were large easy-chairs, silken sofas, large tables full of picture-books and full of toys, worth hundreds and hundreds of crowns—at least the children said so. And the Fir Tree was stuck upright in a cask that was filled with sand; but no one could see that it was a cask, for green cloth was hung all round it, and it stood on a large gaily-colored carpet. Oh! how the Tree quivered! What was to happen? The servants, as well as the young ladies, decorated it. On one branch there hung little nets cut out of colored paper, and each net was filled with sugarplums; and among the other boughs gilded apples and walnuts were suspended, looking as though they had grown there, and little blue and white tapers were placed among the leaves. Dolls that looked for all the world like men—the Tree had never beheld such before—were seen among the foliage, and at the very top a large star of gold tinsel was fixed. It was really splendid—beyond description splendid.

"This evening!" they all said. "How it will shine this evening!"

"Oh!" thought the Tree. "If the evening were but come! If the tapers were but lighted! And then I wonder what will happen! Perhaps the other trees from the forest will come to look at me! Perhaps the sparrows will beat against the windowpanes! I wonder if I shall take root here, and winter and summer stand covered with ornaments!"

He knew very much about the matter—but he was so impatient that for sheer longing he got a pain in his back, and this with trees is the same thing as a headache with us.

The candles were now lighted—what brightness! What splendor! The Tree trembled so in every bough that one of the tapers set fire to the foliage. It blazed up famously.

"Help! Help!" cried the young ladies, and they quickly put out the fire.

Now the Tree did not even dare tremble. What a state he was in! He was so uneasy lest he should lose something of his splendor, that he was quite bewildered amidst the glare and brightness; when suddenly both folding-doors opened and a troop of children rushed in as if they would upset the Tree. The older persons followed quietly; the little ones stood quite still. But it was only for a moment; then they shouted that the whole place re-echoed with their rejoicing; they danced round the Tree, and one present after the other was pulled off.

"What are they about?" thought the Tree. "What is to happen now!" And the lights burned down to the very branches, and as they burned down they were put out one after the other, and then the children had permission to plunder the Tree. So they fell upon it with such violence that all its branches cracked; if it had not been fixed firmly in the ground, it would certainly have tumbled down.

The children danced about with their beautiful playthings; no one looked at the Tree except the old nurse, who peeped between the branches; but it was only to see if there was a fig or an apple left that had been forgotten.

"A story! A story!" cried the children, drawing a little fat man towards the Tree. He seated himself under it and said, "Now we are in the shade, and the Tree can listen too. But I shall tell only one story. Now which will you have; that about Ivedy-Avedy, or about Humpy-Dumpy, who tumbled downstairs, and yet after all came to the throne and married the princess?"

"Ivedy-Avedy," cried some; "Humpy-Dumpy," cried the others. There was such a bawling and screaming—the Fir Tree alone was silent, and he thought to himself, "Am I not to bawl with the rest? Am I to do nothing whatever?" for he was one of the company, and had done what he had to do.

And the man told about Humpy-Dumpy that tumbled down, who notwithstanding came to the throne, and at last married the princess. And the children clapped their hands, and cried. "Oh, go on! Do go on!" They wanted to hear about Ivedy-Avedy too, but the little man only told them about Humpy-Dumpy. The Fir Tree stood quite still and absorbed in thought; the birds in the wood had never related the like of this. "Humpy-Dumpy fell downstairs, and yet he married the princess! Yes, yes! That's the way of the world!" thought the Fir Tree, and believed it all, because the man who told the story was so good-looking. "Well, well! who knows, perhaps I may fall downstairs, too, and get a princess as wife!" And he looked forward with joy to the morrow, when he hoped to be decked out again with lights, playthings, fruits, and tinsel.

"I won't tremble to-morrow!" thought the Fir Tree. "I will enjoy to the full all my splendor! To-morrow I shall hear again the story of Humpy-Dumpy, and perhaps that of Ivedy-Avedy too." And the whole night the Tree stood still and in deep thought.

In the morning the servant and the housemaid came in.

"Now then the splendor will begin again," thought the Fir. But they dragged him out of the room, and up the stairs into the loft: and here, in a dark corner, where no daylight could enter, they left him. "What's the meaning of this?" thought the Tree. "What am I to do here? What shall I hear now, I wonder?" And he leaned against the wall lost in reverie. Time enough had he too for his reflections; for days and nights passed on, and nobody came up; and when at last somebody did come, it was only to put some great trunks in a corner, out of the way. There stood the Tree quite hidden; it seemed as if he had been entirely forgotten.

"'Tis now winter out-of-doors!" thought the Tree. "The earth is hard and covered with snow; men cannot plant me now, and therefore I have been put up here under shelter till the spring-time comes! How thoughtful that is! How kind man is, after all! If it only were not so dark here, and so terribly lonely! Not even a hare! And out in the woods it was so pleasant, when the snow was on the ground, and the hare leaped by; yes—even when he jumped over me; but I did not like it then! It is really terribly lonely here!"

"Squeak! Squeak!" said a little Mouse, at the same moment, peeping out of his hole. And then another little one came. They snuffed about the Fir Tree, and rustled among the branches.

"It is dreadfully cold," said the Mouse. "But for that, it would be delightful here, old Fir, wouldn't it?"

"I am by no means old," said the Fir Tree. "There's many a one considerably older than I am."

"Where do you come from," asked the Mice; "and what can you do?" They were so extremely curious. "Tell us about the most beautiful spot on the earth. Have you never been there? Were you never in the larder, where cheeses lie on the shelves, and hams hang from above; where one dances about on tallow candles: that place where one enters lean, and comes out again fat and portly?"

"I know no such place," said the Tree. "But I know the wood, where the sun shines and where the little birds sing." And then he told all about his youth; and the little Mice had never heard the like before; and they listened and said, "Well, to be sure! How much you have seen! How happy you must have been!"

"I!" said the Fir Tree, thinking over what he had himself related.

"Yes, in reality those were happy times." And then he told about Christmas-eve, when he was decked out with cakes and candles.

"Oh," said the little Mice, "how fortunate you have been, old Fir Tree!"

"I am by no means old," said he. "I came from the wood this winter; I am in my prime, and am only rather short for my age."

"What delightful stories you know," said the Mice: and the next night they came with four other little Mice, who were to hear what the Tree recounted: and the more he related, the more he remembered himself; and it appeared as if those times had really been happy times. "But they may still come—they may still come! Humpy-Dumpy fell downstairs, and yet he got a princess!" and he thought at the moment of a nice little Birch Tree growing out in the woods: to the Fir, that would be a real charming princess.

"Who is Humpy-Dumpy?" asked the Mice. So then the Fir Tree told the whole fairy tale, for he could remember every single word of it; and the little Mice jumped for joy up to the very top of the Tree. Next night two more Mice came, and on Sunday two Rats even; but they said the stories were not interesting, which vexed the little Mice; and they, too, now began to think them not so very amusing either.

"Do you know only one story?" asked the Rats.

"Only that one," answered the Tree. "I heard it on my happiest evening; but I did not then know how happy I was."

"It is a very stupid story! Don't you know one about bacon and tallow candles? Can't you tell any larder stories?"

"No," said the Tree.

"Then good-bye," said the Rats; and they went home.

At last the little Mice stayed away also; and the Tree sighed: "After all, it was very pleasant when the sleek little Mice sat round me, and listened to what I told them. Now that too is over. But I will take good care to enjoy myself when I am brought out again."

But when was that to be? Why, one morning there came a quantity of people and set to work in the loft. The trunks were moved, the tree was pulled out and thrown—rather hard, it is true—down on the floor, but a man drew him towards the stairs, where the daylight shone.

"Now a merry life will begin again," thought the Tree. He felt the fresh air, the first sunbeam—and now he was out in the courtyard. All passed so quickly, there was so much going on around him, the Tree quite forgot to look to himself. The court adjoined a garden, and all was in flower; the roses hung so fresh and odorous over the balustrade, the lindens were in blossom, the Swallows flew by, and said, "Quirre-vit! My husband is come!" but it was not the Fir Tree that they meant.

"Now, then, I shall really enjoy life," said he exultingly, and spread out his branches; but, alas, they were all withered and yellow! It was in a corner that he lay, among weeds and nettles. The golden star of tinsel was still on the top of the Tree, and glittered in the sunshine.

In the court-yard some of the merry children were playing who had danced at Christmas round the Fir Tree, and were so glad at the sight of him. One of the youngest ran and tore off the golden star.

"Only look what is still on the ugly old Christmas tree!" said he, trampling on the branches, so that they all cracked beneath his feet.

And the Tree beheld all the beauty of the flowers, and the freshness in the garden; he beheld himself, and wished he had remained in his dark corner in the loft; he thought of his first youth in the wood, of the merry Christmas-eve, and of the little Mice who had listened with so much pleasure to the story of Humpy-Dumpy.

"'Tis over—'tis past!" said the poor Tree. "Had I but rejoiced when I had reason to do so! But now 'tis past, 'tis past!"

And the gardener's boy chopped the Tree into small pieces; there was a whole heap lying there. The wood flamed up splendidly under the large brewing copper, and it sighed so deeply! Each sigh was like a shot.

The boys played about in the court, and the youngest wore the gold star on his breast which the Tree had had on the happiest evening of his life. However, that was over now—the Tree gone, the story at an end. All, all was over—every tale must end at last.

THE SNOW MAN

By Hans Christian Andersen

"It is so delightfully cold," said the Snow Man, "that it makes my whole body crackle. This is just the kind of wind to blow life into one. How that great red thing up there is staring at me!" He meant the sun, who was just setting. "It shall not make me wink. I shall manage to keep the pieces."

He had two triangular pieces of tile in his head, instead of eyes; his mouth was made of an old broken rake, and was, of course, furnished with teeth. He had been brought into existence amidst the joyous shouts of boys, the jingling of sleigh-bells, and the slashing of whips. The sun went down, and the full moon rose, large, round, and clear, shining in the deep blue.

"There it comes again, from the other side," said the Snow Man, who supposed the sun was showing himself once more. "Ah, I have cured him of staring, though; now he may hang up there, and shine, that I may see myself. If I only knew how to manage to move away from this place,- I should so like to move. If I could, I would slide along yonder on the ice, as I have seen the boys do; but I don't understand how; I don't even know how to run."

"Away, away," barked the old yard-dog. He was quite hoarse, and could not pronounce "Bow wow" properly. He had once been an indoor dog, and lay by the fire, and he had been hoarse ever since. "The sun will make you run some day. I saw him, last winter, make your predecessor run, and his predecessor before him. Away, away, they all have to go."

"I don't understand you, comrade," said the Snow Man. "Is that thing up yonder to teach me to run? I saw it running itself a little while ago, and now it has come creeping up from the other side."

"You know nothing at all," replied the yard-dog; "but then, you've only lately been patched up. What you see yonder is the moon, and the one before it was the sun. It will come again to-morrow, and most likely teach you to run down into the ditch by the well; for I think the weather is going to change. I can feel such pricks and stabs in my left leg; I am sure there is going to be a change."

"I don't understand him," said the Snow Man to himself; "but I have a feeling that he is talking of something very disagreeable. The one who stared so just now, and whom he calls the sun, is not my friend; I can feel that too."

"Away, away," barked the yard-dog, and then he turned round three times, and crept into his kennel to sleep.

There was really a change in the weather. Towards morning, a thick fog covered the whole country round, and a keen wind arose, so that the cold seemed to freeze one's bones; but when the sun rose, the sight was splendid. Trees and bushes were covered with hoar frost, and looked like a forest of white coral; while on every twig glittered frozen dew-drops. The many delicate forms concealed in summer by luxuriant foliage, were now clearly defined, and looked like glittering lace-work. From every twig glistened a white radiance. The birch, waving in the wind, looked full of life, like trees in summer; and its appearance was wondrously beautiful. And where the sun shone, how everything glittered and sparkled, as if diamond dust had been strewn about; while the snowy carpet of the earth appeared as if covered with diamonds, from which countless lights gleamed, whiter than even the snow itself.

"This is really beautiful," said a young girl, who had come into the garden with a young man; and they both stood still near the Snow Man, and contemplated the glittering scene. "Summer cannot show a more beautiful sight," she exclaimed, while her eyes sparkled.

"And we can't have such a fellow as this in the summer time," replied the young man, pointing to the Snow Man; "he is capital."

The girl laughed, and nodded at the Snow Man, and then tripped away over the snow with her friend. The snow creaked and crackled beneath her feet, as if she had been treading on starch.

"Who are these two?" asked the Snow Man of the yard-dog. "You have been here longer than I have; do you know them?"

"Of course I know them," replied the yard-dog; "she has stroked my back many times, and he has given me a bone of meat. I never bite those two."

"But what are they?" asked the Snow Man.

"They are lovers," he replied; "they will go and live in the same kennel by-and-by, and gnaw at the same bone. Away, away!"

"Are they the same kind of beings as you and I?" asked the Snow Man.

"Well, they belong to the same master," retorted the yard-dog. "Certainly people who were only born yesterday know very little. I can see that in you. I have age and experience. I know every one here in the house, and I know there was once a time when I did not lie out here in the cold, fastened to a chain. Away, away!"

"The cold is delightful," said the Snow Man; "but do tell me tell me; only you must not clank your chain so; for it jars all through me when you do that."

"Away, away!" barked the yard-dog; "I'll tell you; they said I was a pretty little fellow once; then I used to lie in a velvet-covered chair, up at the master's house, and sit in the mistress's lap. They used to kiss my nose, and wipe my paws with an embroidered handkerchief, and I was called 'Ami, dear Ami, sweet Ami.' But after a while I grew too big for them, and they sent me away to the housekeeper's room; so I came to live on the lower story. You can look into the room from where you stand, and see where I was master once; for I was indeed master to the housekeeper. It was certainly a smaller room than those up stairs; but I was more comfortable; for I was not being continually taken hold of and pulled about by the children as I had been. I received quite as good food, or even better. I had my own cushion, and there was a stove- it is the finest thing in the world at this season of the year. I used to go under the stove, and lie down quite beneath it. Ah, I still dream of that stove. Away, away!"

"Does a stove look beautiful?" asked the Snow Man, "is it at all like me?"

"It is just the reverse of you,' said the dog; "it's as black as a crow, and has a long neck and a brass knob; it eats firewood, so that fire spurts out of its mouth. We should keep on one side, or under it, to be comfortable. You can see it through the window, from where you stand."

Then the Snow Man looked, and saw a bright polished thing with a brazen knob, and fire gleaming from the lower part of it. The Snow Man felt quite a strange sensation come over him; it was very odd, he knew not what it meant, and he could not account for it. But there are people who are not men of snow, who understand what it is. "'And why did you leave her?" asked the Snow Man, for it seemed to him that the stove must be of the female sex. "How could you give up such a comfortable place?"

"I was obliged," replied the yard-dog. "They turned me out of doors, and chained me up here. I had bitten the youngest of my master's sons in the leg, because he kicked away the bone I was gnawing. 'Bone for bone,' I thought; but they were so angry, and from that time I have been fastened with a chain, and lost my bone. Don't you hear how hoarse I am. Away, away! I can't talk any more like other dogs. Away, away, that is the end of it all."

But the Snow Man was no longer listening. He was looking into the housekeeper's room on the lower storey; where the stove stood on its four iron legs, looking about the same size as the Snow Man himself. "What a strange crackling I feel within me," he said. "Shall I ever get in there? It is an innocent wish, and innocent wishes are sure to be fulfilled. I must go in there and lean against her, even if I have to break the window."

"You must never go in there," said the yard-dog, "for if you approach the stove, you'll melt away, away."

"I might as well go," said the Snow Man, "for I think I am breaking up as it is."

During the whole day the Snow Man stood looking in through the window, and in the twilight hour the room became still more inviting, for from the stove came a gentle glow, not like the sun or the moon; no, only the bright light which gleams from a stove when it has been well fed. When the door of the stove was opened, the flames darted out of its mouth; this is customary with all stoves. The light of the flames fell directly on the face and breast of the Snow Man with a ruddy gleam. "I can endure it no longer," said he; "how beautiful it looks when it stretches out its tongue?"

The night was long, but did not appear so to the Snow Man, who stood there enjoying his own reflections, and crackling with the cold. In the morning, the window-panes of the housekeeper's room were covered with ice. They were the most beautiful ice-flowers any Snow Man could desire, but they concealed the stove. These window-panes would not thaw, and he could see nothing of the stove, which he pictured to himself, as if it had been a lovely human being. The snow crackled and the wind whistled around him; it was just the kind of frosty weather a Snow Man might thoroughly enjoy. But he did not enjoy it; how, indeed, could he enjoy anything when he was "stove sick?"

"That is terrible disease for a Snow Man," said the yard-dog; "I have suffered from it myself, but I got over it. Away, away," he barked and then he added, "the weather is going to change." And the weather did change; it began to thaw. As the warmth increased, the Snow Man decreased. He said nothing and made no complaint, which is a sure sign. One morning he broke, and sunk down altogether; and, behold, where he had stood, something like a broomstick remained sticking up in the ground. It was the pole round which the boys had built him up. "Ah, now I understand why he had such a great longing for the stove," said the yard-dog. "Why, there's the shovel that is used for cleaning out the stove, fastened to the pole." The Snow Man had a stove scraper in his body; that was what moved him so. "But it's all over now. Away, away." And soon the winter passed. "Away, away," barked the hoarse yard-dog. But the girls in the house sang,

> "Come from your fragrant home, green thyme;
> Stretch your soft branches, willow-tree;
> The months are bringing the sweet spring-time,
> When the lark in the sky sings joyfully.
> Come gentle sun, while the cuckoo sings,
> And I'll mock his note in my wanderings."

And nobody thought any more of the Snow Man.

THE END

A KIDNAPPED SANTA CLAUS

By L. Frank Baum

Santa Claus lives in the Laughing Valley, where stands the big, rambling castle in which his toys are manufactured. His workmen, selected from the ryls, knooks, pixies and fairies, live with him, and every one is as busy as can be from one year's end to another.

It is called the Laughing Valley because everything there is happy and gay. The brook chuckles to itself as it leaps rollicking between its green banks; the wind whistles merrily in the trees; the sunbeams dance lightly over the soft grass, and the violets and wild flowers look smilingly up from their green nests. To laugh one needs to be happy; to be happy one needs to be content. And throughout the Laughing Valley of Santa Claus contentment reigns supreme.

On one side is the mighty Forest of Burzee. At the other side stands the huge mountain that contains the Caves of the Daemons. And between them the Valley lies smiling and peaceful.

One would think that our good old Santa Claus, who devotes his days to making children happy, would have no enemies on all the earth; and, as a matter of fact, for a long period of time he encountered nothing but love wherever he might go.

But the Daemons who live in the mountain caves grew to hate Santa Claus very much, and all for the simple reason that he made children happy.

The Caves of the Daemons are five in number. A broad pathway leads up to the first cave, which is a finely arched cavern at the foot of the mountain, the entrance being beautifully carved and decorated. In it resides the Daemon of Selfishness. Back of this is another cavern inhabited by the Daemon of Envy. The cave of the Daemon of Hatred is next in order, and through this one passes to the home of the Daemon of Malice--situated in a dark and fearful cave in the very heart of the mountain. I do not know what lies beyond this. Some say there are terrible pitfalls leading to death and destruction, and this may very well be true. However, from each one of the four caves mentioned there is a small, narrow tunnel leading to the fifth cave--a cozy little room occupied by the Daemon of Repentance. And as the rocky floors of these passages are well worn by the track of passing feet, I judge that many wanderers in the Caves of the Daemons have escaped through the tunnels to the abode of the Daemon of Repentance, who is said to be a pleasant sort of fellow who gladly opens for one a little door admitting you into fresh air and sunshine again.

Well, these Daemons of the Caves, thinking they had great cause to dislike old Santa Claus, held a meeting one day to discuss the matter.

"I'm really getting lonesome," said the Daemon of Selfishness. "For Santa Claus distributes so many pretty Christmas gifts to all the children that they become happy and generous, through his example, and keep away from my cave."

"I'm having the same trouble," rejoined the Daemon of Envy. "The little ones seem quite content with Santa Claus, and there are few, indeed, that I can coax to become envious."

"And that makes it bad for me!" declared the Daemon of Hatred. "For if no children pass through the Caves of Selfishness and Envy, none can get to MY cavern."

"Or to mine," added the Daemon of Malice.

"For my part," said the Daemon of Repentance, "it is easily seen that if children do not visit your caves they have no need to visit mine; so that I am quite as neglected as you are."

"And all because of this person they call Santa Claus!" exclaimed the Daemon of Envy. "He is simply ruining our business, and something must be done at once."

To this they readily agreed; but what to do was another and more difficult matter to settle. They knew that Santa Claus worked all through the year at his castle in the Laughing Valley, preparing the gifts he was to distribute on Christmas Eve; and at first they resolved to try to tempt him into their caves, that they might lead him on to the terrible pitfalls that ended in destruction.

So the very next day, while Santa Claus was busily at work, surrounded by his little band of assistants, the Daemon of Selfishness came to him and said:

"These toys are wonderfully bright and pretty. Why do you not keep them for yourself? It's a pity to give them to those noisy boys and fretful girls, who break and destroy them so quickly.

"Nonsense!" cried the old graybeard, his bright eyes twinkling merrily as he turned toward the tempting Daemon. "The boys and girls are never so noisy and fretful after receiving my presents, and if I can make them happy for one day in the year I am quite content."

So the Daemon went back to the others, who awaited him in their caves, and said:

"I have failed, for Santa Claus is not at all selfish."

The following day the Daemon of Envy visited Santa Claus. Said he: "The toy shops are full of playthings quite as pretty as those you are making. What a shame it is that they should interfere with your business! They make toys by machinery much quicker than you can make them by hand; and they sell them for money, while you get nothing at all for your work."

But Santa Claus refused to be envious of the toy shops.

"I can supply the little ones but once a year--on Christmas Eve," he answered; "for the children are many, and I am but one. And as my work is one of love and kindness I would be ashamed to receive money for my little gifts. But throughout all the year the children must be amused in some way, and so the toy shops are able to bring much happiness to my little friends. I like the toy shops, and am glad to see them prosper."

In spite of the second rebuff, the Daemon of Hatred thought he would try to influence Santa Claus. So the next day he entered the busy workshop and said:

"Good morning, Santa! I have bad news for you."

"Then run away, like a good fellow," answered Santa Claus. "Bad news is something that should be kept secret and never told."

"You cannot escape this, however," declared the Daemon; "for in the world are a good many who do not believe in Santa Claus, and these you are bound to hate bitterly, since they have so wronged you."

"Stuff and rubbish!" cried Santa.

"And there are others who resent your making children happy and who sneer at you and call you a foolish old rattlepate! You are quite right to hate such base slanderers, and you ought to be revenged upon them for their evil words."

"But I don't hate 'em!" exclaimed Santa Claus positively. "Such people do me no real harm, but merely render themselves and their children unhappy. Poor things! I'd much rather help them any day than injure them."

Indeed, the Daemons could not tempt old Santa Claus in any way. On the contrary, he was shrewd enough to see that their object in visiting him was to make mischief and trouble, and his cheery laughter disconcerted the evil ones and showed to them the folly of such an undertaking. So they abandoned honeyed words and determined to use force.

It was well known that no harm can come to Santa Claus while he is in the Laughing Valley, for the fairies, and ryls, and knooks all protect him. But on Christmas Eve he drives his reindeer out into the big world, carrying a sleighload of toys and pretty gifts to the children; and this was the time and the occasion when his enemies had the best chance to injure him. So the Daemons laid their plans and awaited the arrival of Christmas Eve.

The moon shone big and white in the sky, and the snow lay crisp and sparkling on the ground as Santa Claus cracked his whip and sped away out of the Valley into the great world beyond. The roomy sleigh was packed full with huge sacks of toys, and as the reindeer dashed onward our jolly old Santa laughed and whistled and sang for very joy. For in all his merry life this was the one day in the year when he was happiest--the day he lovingly bestowed the treasures of his workshop upon the little children.

It would be a busy night for him, he well knew. As he whistled and shouted and cracked his whip again, he reviewed in mind all the towns and cities and farmhouses where he was expected, and figured that he had just enough presents to go around and make every child happy. The reindeer knew exactly what was expected of them, and dashed along so swiftly that their feet scarcely seemed to touch the snow-covered ground.

Suddenly a strange thing happened: a rope shot through the moonlight and a big noose that was in the end of it settled over the arms and body of Santa Claus and drew tight. Before he could resist or even cry out he was jerked from the seat of the sleigh and tumbled head foremost into a snowbank, while the reindeer rushed onward with the load of toys and carried it quickly out of sight and sound.

Such a surprising experience confused old Santa for a moment, and when he had collected his senses he found that the wicked Daemons had pulled him from the snowdrift and bound him tightly with many coils of the stout rope. And then they carried the kidnapped Santa Claus away to their mountain, where they thrust the prisoner into a secret cave and chained him to the rocky wall so that he could not escape.

"Ha, ha!" laughed the Daemons, rubbing their hands together with cruel glee. "What will the children do now? How they will cry and scold and storm when they find there are no toys in their stockings and no gifts on their Christmas trees! And what a lot of punishment they will receive from their parents, and how they will flock to our Caves of Selfishness, and Envy, and Hatred, and Malice! We have done a mighty clever thing, we Daemons of the Caves!"

Now it so chanced that on this Christmas Eve the good Santa Claus had taken with him in his sleigh Nuter the Ryl, Peter the Knook, Kilter the Pixie, and a small fairy named Wisk--his four favorite assistants. These little people he had often found very useful in helping him to distribute his gifts to the children, and when their master was so suddenly dragged from the sleigh they were all snugly tucked underneath the seat, where the sharp wind could not reach them.

The tiny immortals knew nothing of the capture of Santa Claus until some time after he had disappeared. But finally they missed his cheery voice, and as their master always sang or whistled on his journeys, the silence warned them that something was wrong.

Little Wisk stuck out his head from underneath the seat and found Santa Claus gone and no one to direct the flight of the reindeer.

"Whoa!" he called out, and the deer obediently slackened speed and came to a halt.

Peter and Nuter and Kilter all jumped upon the seat and looked back over the track made by the sleigh. But Santa Claus had been left miles and miles behind.

"What shall we do?" asked Wisk anxiously, all the mirth and mischief banished from his wee face by this great calamity.

"We must go back at once and find our master," said Nuter the Ryl, who thought and spoke with much deliberation.

"No, no!" exclaimed Peter the Knook, who, cross and crabbed though he was, might always be depended upon in an emergency. "If we delay, or go back, there will not be time to get the toys to the children before morning; and that would grieve Santa Claus more than anything else."

"It is certain that some wicked creatures have captured him," added Kilter thoughtfully, "and their object must be to make the children unhappy. So our first duty is to get the toys distributed as carefully as if Santa Claus were himself present. Afterward we can search for our master and easily secure his freedom."

This seemed such good and sensible advice that the others at once resolved to adopt it. So Peter the Knook called to the reindeer, and the faithful animals again sprang forward and dashed over hill and valley, through forest and plain, until they came to the houses wherein children lay sleeping and dreaming of the pretty gifts they would find on Christmas morning.

The little immortals had set themselves a difficult task; for although they had assisted Santa Claus on many of his journeys, their master had always directed and guided them and told them exactly what he wished them to do. But now they had to distribute the toys according to their own judgment, and they did not understand children as well as did old Santa. So it is no wonder they made some laughable errors.

Mamie Brown, who wanted a doll, got a drum instead; and a drum is of no use to a girl who loves dolls. And Charlie Smith, who delights to romp and play out of doors, and who wanted some new rubber boots to keep his feet dry, received a sewing box filled with colored worsteds and threads and needles, which made him so provoked that he thoughtlessly called our dear Santa Claus a fraud.

Had there been many such mistakes the Daemons would have accomplished their evil purpose and made the children unhappy. But the little friends of the absent Santa Claus labored faithfully and intelligently to carry out their master's ideas, and they made fewer errors than might be expected under such unusual circumstances.

And, although they worked as swiftly as possible, day had begun to break before the toys and other presents were all distributed; so for the first time in many years the reindeer trotted into the Laughing Valley, on their return, in broad daylight, with the brilliant sun peeping over the edge of the forest to prove they were far behind their accustomed hours.

Having put the deer in the stable, the little folk began to wonder how they might rescue their master; and they realized they must discover, first of all, what had happened to him and where he was.

So Wisk the Fairy transported himself to the bower of the Fairy Queen, which was located deep in the heart of the Forest of Burzee; and once there, it did not take him long to find out all about the naughty Daemons and how they had kidnapped the good Santa Claus to prevent his making children happy. The Fairy Queen also promised her assistance, and then, fortified by this powerful support, Wisk flew back to where Nuter and Peter and Kilter awaited him, and the four counseled together and laid plans to rescue their master from his enemies.

It is possible that Santa Claus was not as merry as usual during the night that succeeded his capture. For although he had faith in the judgment of his little friends he could not avoid a certain amount of worry, and an anxious look would creep at times into his kind old eyes as he thought of the disappointment that might await his dear little children. And the Daemons, who guarded him by turns, one after another, did not neglect to taunt him with contemptuous words in his helpless condition.

When Christmas Day dawned the Daemon of Malice was guarding the prisoner, and his tongue was sharper than that of any of the others.

"The children are waking up, Santa!" he cried. "They are waking up to find their stockings empty! Ho, ho! How they will quarrel, and wail, and stamp their feet in anger! Our caves will be full today, old Santa! Our caves are sure to be full!"

But to this, as to other like taunts, Santa Claus answered nothing. He was much grieved by his capture, it is true; but his courage did not forsake him. And, finding that the prisoner would not reply to his jeers, the Daemon of Malice presently went away, and sent the Daemon of Repentance to take his place.

This last personage was not so disagreeable as the others. He had gentle and refined features, and his voice was soft and pleasant in tone.

"My brother Daemons do not trust me overmuch," said he, as he entered the cavern; "but it is morning, now, and the mischief is done. You cannot visit the children again for another year."

"That is true," answered Santa Claus, almost cheerfully; "Christmas Eve is past, and for the first time in centuries I have not visited my children."

"The little ones will be greatly disappointed," murmured the Daemon of Repentance, almost regretfully; "but that cannot be helped now. Their grief is likely to make the children selfish and envious and hateful, and if they come to the Caves of the Daemons today I shall get a chance to lead some of them to my Cave of Repentance."

"Do you never repent, yourself?" asked Santa Claus, curiously.

"Oh, yes, indeed," answered the Daemon. "I am even now repenting that I assisted in your capture. Of course it is too late to remedy the evil that has been done; but repentance, you know, can come only after an evil thought or deed, for in the beginning there is nothing to repent of."

"So I understand," said Santa Claus. "Those who avoid evil need never visit your cave."

"As a rule, that is true," replied the Daemon; "yet you, who have done no evil, are about to visit my cave at once; for to prove that I sincerely regret my share in your capture I am going to permit you to escape."

This speech greatly surprised the prisoner, until he reflected that it was just what might be expected of the Daemon of Repentance. The fellow at once busied himself untying the knots that bound Santa Claus and unlocking the chains that fastened him to the wall. Then he led the way through a long tunnel until they both emerged in the Cave of Repentance.

"I hope you will forgive me," said the Daemon pleadingly. "I am not really a bad person, you know; and I believe I accomplish a great deal of good in the world."

With this he opened a back door that let in a flood of sunshine, and Santa Claus sniffed the fresh air gratefully.

"I bear no malice," said he to the Daemon, in a gentle voice; "and I am sure the world would be a dreary place without you. So, good morning, and a Merry Christmas to you!"

With these words he stepped out to greet the bright morning, and a moment later he was trudging along, whistling softly to himself, on his way to his home in the Laughing Valley.

Marching over the snow toward the mountain was a vast army, made up of the most curious creatures imaginable. There were numberless knooks from the forest, as rough and crooked in appearance as the gnarled branches of the trees they ministered to. And there were dainty ryls from the fields, each one bearing the emblem of the flower or plant it guarded. Behind these were many ranks of pixies, gnomes and nymphs, and in the rear a thousand beautiful fairies floated along in gorgeous array.

This wonderful army was led by Wisk, Peter, Nuter, and Kilter, who had assembled it to rescue Santa Claus from captivity and to punish the Daemons who had dared to take him away from his beloved children.

And, although they looked so bright and peaceful, the little immortals were armed with powers that would be very terrible to those who had incurred their anger. Woe to the Daemons of the Caves if this mighty army of vengeance ever met them!

But lo! coming to meet his loyal friends appeared the imposing form of Santa Claus, his white beard floating in the breeze and his bright eyes sparkling with pleasure at this proof of the love and veneration he had inspired in the hearts of the most powerful creatures in existence.

And while they clustered around him and danced with glee at his safe return, he gave them earnest thanks for their support. But Wisk, and Nuter, and Peter, and Kilter, he embraced affectionately.

"It is useless to pursue the Daemons," said Santa Claus to the army. "They have their place in the world, and can never be destroyed. But that is a great pity, nevertheless," he continued musingly.

So the fairies, and knooks, and pixies, and ryls all escorted the good man to his castle, and there left him to talk over the events of the night with his little assistants.

Wisk had already rendered himself invisible and flown through the big world to see how the children were getting along on this bright Christmas morning; and by the time he returned, Peter had finished telling Santa Claus of how they had distributed the toys.

"We really did very well," cried the fairy, in a pleased voice; "for I found little unhappiness among the children this morning. Still, you must not get captured again, my dear master; for we might not be so fortunate another time in carrying out your ideas."

He then related the mistakes that had been made, and which he had not discovered until his tour of inspection. And Santa Claus at once sent him with rubber boots for Charlie Smith, and a doll for Mamie Brown; so that even those two disappointed ones became happy.

As for the wicked Daemons of the Caves, they were filled with anger and chagrin when they found that their clever capture of Santa Claus had come to naught. Indeed, no one on that Christmas Day appeared to be at all selfish, or envious, or hateful. And, realizing that while the children's saint had so many powerful friends it was folly to oppose him, the Daemons never again attempted to interfere with his journeys on Christmas Eve.

LITTLE BUN RABBIT

By L. Frank Baum

"Oh, Little Bun Rabbit, so soft and so shy,
Say, what do you see with your big, round eye?"
"On Christmas we rabbits," says Bunny so shy,
"Keep watch to see Santa go galloping by."

Little Dorothy had passed all the few years of her life in the country, and being the only child upon the farm she was allowed to roam about the meadows and woods as she pleased. On the bright summer mornings Dorothy's mother would tie a sun-bonnet under the girl's chin, and then she romped away to the fields to amuse herself in her own way.

She came to know every flower that grew, and to call them by name, and she always stepped very carefully to avoid treading on them, for Dorothy was a kind-hearted child and did not like to crush the pretty flowers that bloomed in her path. And she was also very fond of all the animals, and learned to know them well, and even to understand their language, which very few people can do. And the animals loved Dorothy in turn, for the word passed around amongst them that she could be trusted to do them no harm. For the horse, whose soft nose Dorothy often gently stroked, told the cow of her kindness, and the cow told the dog, and the dog told the cat, and the cat told her black kitten, and the black kitten told the rabbit when one day they met in the turnip patch.

Therefore when the rabbit, which is the most timid of all animals and the most difficult to get acquainted with, looked out of a small bush at the edge of the wood one day and saw Dorothy standing a little way off, he did not scamper away, as is his custom, but sat very still and met the gaze of her sweet eyes boldly, although perhaps his heart beat a little faster than usual.

Dorothy herself was afraid she might frighten him away, so she kept very quiet for a time, leaning silently against a tree and smiling encouragement at her timorous companion until the rabbit became reassured and blinked his big eyes at her thoughtfully. For he was as much interested in the little girl as she in him, since it was the first time he had dared to meet a person face to face.

Finally Dorothy ventured to speak, so she asked, very softly and slowly,

"Oh, Little Bun Rabbit, so soft and so shy,
Say, what do you see with your big, round eye?"

"Many things," answered the rabbit, who was pleased to hear the girl speak in his own language; "in summer-time I see the clover-leaves that I love to feed upon and the cabbages at the end of the farmer's garden. I see the cool bushes where I can hide from my enemies, and I see the dogs and the men long before they can see me, or know that I am near, and therefore I am able to keep out of their way."

"Is that the reason your eyes are so big?" asked Dorothy.

"I suppose so," returned the rabbit; "you see we have only our eyes and our ears and our legs to defend ourselves with. We cannot fight, but we can always run away, and that is a much better way to save our lives than by fighting."

"Where is your home, bunny?" enquired the girl.

"I live in the ground, far down in a cool, pleasant hole I have dug in the midst of the forest. At the bottom of the hole is the nicest little room you can imagine, and there I have made a soft bed to rest in at night. When I meet an enemy I run to my hole and jump in, and there I stay until all danger is over."

"You have told me what you see in summer," continued Dorothy, who was greatly interested in the rabbit's account of himself, "but what do you see in the winter?"

"In winter we rabbits," said Bunny so shy, "Keep watch to see Santa go galloping by."

"And do you ever see him?" asked the girl, eagerly.

"Oh, yes; every winter. I am not afraid of him, nor of his reindeer. And it is such fun to see him come dashing along, cracking his whip and calling out cheerily to his reindeer, who are able to run even swifter than we rabbits. And Santa Claus, when he sees me, always gives me a nod and a smile, and then I look after him and his big load of toys which he is carrying to the children, until he has galloped away out of sight. I like to see the toys, for they are so bright and pretty, and every year there is something new amongst them. Once I visited Santa, and saw him make the toys."

"Oh, tell me about it!" pleaded Dorothy.

"It was one morning after Christmas," said the rabbit, who seemed to enjoy talking, now that he had overcome his fear of

Dorothy, "and I was sitting by the road-side when Santa Claus came riding back in his empty sleigh. He does not come home quite so fast as he goes, and when he saw me he stopped for a word.

"'You look very pretty this morning, Bun Rabbit,' he said, in his jolly way; 'I think the babies would love to have you to play with.'

"'I don't doubt it, your honor,' I answered; 'but they 'd soon kill me with handling, even if they did not scare me to death; for babies are very rough with their playthings.'

"'That is true,' replied Santa Claus; 'and yet you are so soft and pretty it is a pity the babies can't have you. Still, as they would abuse a live rabbit I think I shall make them some toy rabbits, which they cannot hurt; so if you will jump into my sleigh with me and ride home to my castle for a few days, I 'll see if I can't make some toy rabbits just like you."

"Of course I consented, for we all like to please old Santa, and a minute later I had jumped into the sleigh beside him and we were dashing away at full speed toward his castle. I enjoyed the ride very much, but I enjoyed the castle far more; for it was one of the loveliest places you could imagine. It stood on the top of a high mountain and is built of gold and silver bricks, and the windows are pure diamond crystals. The rooms are big and high, and there is a soft carpet upon every floor and many strange things scattered around to amuse one. Santa Claus lives there all alone, except for old Mother Hubbard, who cooks the meals for him; and her cupboard is never bare now, I can promise you! At the top of the castle there is one big room, and that is Santa's work-shop, where he makes the toys. On one side is his work-bench, with plenty of saws and hammers and jack-knives; and on another side is the paint-bench, with paints of every color and brushes of every size and shape. And in other places are great shelves, where the toys are put to dry and keep new and bright until Christmas comes and it is time to load them all into his sleigh.

"After Mother Hubbard had given me a good dinner, and I had eaten some of the most delicious clover I have ever tasted, Santa took me up into his work-room and sat me upon the table.

"'If I can only make rabbits half as nice as you are,' he said, 'the little ones will be delighted.' Then he lit a big pipe and began to smoke, and soon he took a roll of soft fur from a shelf in a corner and commenced to cut it out in the shape of a rabbit. He smoked and whistled all the time he was working, and he talked to me in such a jolly way that I sat perfectly still and allowed him to measure my ears and my legs so that he could cut the fur into the proper form.

"'Why, I 've got your nose too long, Bunny,' he said once; and so he snipped a little off the fur he was cutting, so that the toy rabbit's nose should be like mine. And again he said, 'Good gracious! the ears are too short entirely!' So he had to get a needle and thread and sew on more fur to the ears, so that they might be the right size. But after a time it was all finished, and then he stuffed the fur full of sawdust and sewed it up neatly; after which he put in some glass eyes that made the toy rabbit look wonderfully life-like. When it was all done he put it on the table beside me, and at first I didn't know whether I was the live rabbit or the toy rabbit, we were so much alike.

"'It's a very good job,' said Santa, nodding his head at us pleasantly; 'and I shall have to make a lot of these rabbits, for the little children are sure to be greatly pleased with them.'

"So he immediately began to make another, and this time he cut the fur just the right size, so that it was even better than the first rabbit.

"'I must put a squeak in it,' said Santa.

"So he took a box of squeaks from a shelf and put one into the rabbit before he sewed it up. When it was all finished he pressed the toy rabbit with his thumb, and it squeaked so naturally that I jumped off the table, fearing at first the new rabbit was alive. Old Santa laughed merrily at this, and I soon recovered from my fright and was pleased to think the babies were to have such pretty playthings.

"'After this,' said Santa Claus, 'I can make rabbits without having you for a pattern; but if you like you may stay a few days longer in my castle and amuse yourself.'"

"I thanked him and decided to stay. So for several days I watched him making all kinds of toys, and I wondered to see how quickly he made them, and how many new things he invented.

"'I almost wish I was a child,' I said to him one day, 'for then I too could have playthings.'

"'Ah, you can run about all day, in summer and in winter, and enjoy yourself in your own way,' said Santa; 'but the poor little children are obliged to stay in the house in the winter and on rainy days in the summer, and then they must have toys to amuse them and keep them contented."

"I knew this was true, so I only said, admiringly, 'You must be the quickest and the best workman in all the world, Santa.'

"'I suppose I am,' he answered; 'but then, you see, I have been making toys for hundreds of years, and I make so many it is no wonder I am skillful. And now, if you are ready to go home, I'll hitch up the reindeer and take you back again.'

"'Oh, no,' said I, 'I prefer to run by myself, for I can easily find the way and I want to see the country.'

"'If that is the case,' replied Santa, 'I must give you a magic collar to wear, so that you will come to no harm.'

"So, after Mother Hubbard had given me a good meal of turnips and sliced cabbage, Santa Claus put the magic collar around my neck and I started for home. I took my time on the journey, for I knew nothing could harm me, and I saw a good many strange sights before I got back to this place again."

"But what became of the magic collar?" asked Dorothy, who had listened with breathless interest to the rabbit's story.

"After I got home," replied the rabbit, "the collar disappeared from around my neck, and I knew Santa had called it back to himself again. He did not give it to me, you see; he merely let me take it on my journey to protect me. The next Christmas, when I watched by the road-side to see Santa, I was pleased to notice a great many of the toy rabbits sticking out of the loaded sleigh. The babies must have liked them, too, for every year since I have seen them amongst the toys.

"Santa never forgets me, and every time he passes he calls out, in his jolly voice,

"'A merry Christmas to you, Bun Rabbit! The babies still love you dearly.'"

The Rabbit paused, and Dorothy was just about to ask another question when Bunny raised his head and seemed to hear something coming.

"What is it?" enquired the girl.

"It's the farmer's big shepherd dog," answered the Rabbit, "and I must be going before he sees me, or I shall shall [both shalls in original] have to run for my life. So good bye, Dorothy; I hope we shall meet again, and then I will gladly tell you more of my adventures."

The next instant he had sprung into the wood, and all that Dorothy could see of him was a gray streak darting in and out amongst the trees.

LITTLE GRETCHEN AND THE WOODEN SHOE

Elizabeth Harrison

The following story is one of many which has drifted down to us from the story-loving nurseries and hearthstones of Germany. I cannot recall when I first had it told to me as a child, varied, of course, by different tellers, but always leaving that sweet, tender impression of God's loving care for the least of his children. I have since read different versions of it in at least a half-dozen story books for children.

Once upon a time, a long time ago, far away across the great ocean, in a country called Germany, there could be seen a small log hut on the edge of a great forest, whose fir-trees extended for miles and miles to the north. This little house, made of heavy hewn logs, had but one room in it. A rough pine door gave entrance to this room, and a small square window admitted the light. At the back of the house was built an old-fashioned stone chimney, out of which in winter usually curled a thin, blue smoke, showing that there was not very much fire within.

Small as the house was, it was large enough for the two people who lived in it. I want to tell you a story to-day about these two people. One was an old, gray-haired woman, so old that the little children of the village, nearly half a mile away, often wondered whether she had come into the world with the huge mountains, and the great fir-trees, which stood like giants back of her small hut. Her face was wrinkled all over with deep lines, which, if the children could only have read aright, would have told them of many years of cheerful, happy, self-sacrifice, of loving, anxious watching beside sick-beds, of quiet endurance of pain, of many a day of hunger and cold, and of a thousand deeds of unselfish love for other people; but, of course, they could not read this strange handwriting. They only knew that she was old and wrinkled, and that she stooped as she walked. None of them seemed to fear her, for her smile was always cheerful, and she had a kindly word for each of them if they chanced to meet her on her way to and from the village. With this old, old woman lived a very little girl. So bright and happy was she that the travellers who passed by the lonesome little house on the edge of the forest often thought of a sunbeam as they saw her. These two people were known in the village as Granny Goodyear and Little Gretchen.

The winter had come and the frost had snapped off many of the smaller branches from the pine-trees in the forest. Gretchen and her Granny were up by daybreak each morning. After their simple breakfast of oatmeal, Gretchen would run to the little closet and fetch Granny's old woollen shawl, which seemed almost as old as Granny herself. Gretchen always claimed the right to put the shawl over her Granny's head, even though she had to climb onto the wooden bench to do it. After carefully pinning it under Granny's chin, she gave her a good-bye kiss, and Granny started out for her morning's work in the forest. This work was nothing more nor less than the gathering up of the twigs and branches which the autumn winds and winter frosts had thrown upon the ground. These were carefully gathered into a large bundle which Granny tied together with a strong linen band. She then managed to lift the bundle to her shoulder and trudged off to the village with it. Here she sold the fagots for kindling wood to the people of the village. Sometimes she would get only a few pence each day, and sometimes a dozen or more, but on this money little Gretchen and she managed to live; they had their home, and the forest kindly furnished the wood for the fire which kept them warm in cold weather.

In the summer time Granny had a little garden at the back of the hut where she raised, with little Gretchen's help, a few potatoes and turnips and onions. These she carefully stored away for winter use. To this meagre supply, the pennies, gained by selling the twigs from the forest, added the oatmeal for Gretchen and a little black coffee for Granny. Meat was a thing they never thought of having. It cost too much money. Still, Granny and Gretchen were very happy, because they loved each other dearly. Sometimes Gretchen would be left alone all day long in the hut, because Granny would have some work to do in the village after selling her bundle of sticks and twigs. It was during these long days that little Gretchen had taught herself to sing the song which the wind sang to the pine branches. In the summer time she learned the chirp and twitter of the birds, until her voice might almost be mistaken for a bird's voice; she learned to dance as the swaying shadows did, and even to talk to the stars which shone through the little square window when Granny came home too late or too tired to talk.

Sometimes, when the weather was fine, or her Granny had an extra bundle of newly knitted stockings to take to the village, she would let little Gretchen go along with her. It chanced that one of these trips to the town came just the week before Christmas, and Gretchen's eyes were delighted by the sight of the lovely Christmas-trees which stood in the window of the village store. It seemed to her that she would never tire of looking at the knit dolls, the woolly lambs, the little wooden shops with their queer, painted men and women in them, and all the other fine things. She had never owned a plaything in her whole life; therefore, toys which you and I would not think much of, seemed to her to be very beautiful.

That night, after their supper of baked potatoes was over, and little Gretchen had cleared away the dishes and swept up the hearth, because Granny dear was so tired, she brought her own small wooden stool and placed it very near Granny's feet and sat down upon it, folding her hands on her lap. Granny knew that this meant she wanted to talk about something, so she smilingly laid away the large Bible which she had been reading, and took up her knitting, which was as much as to say: "Well, Gretchen, dear, Granny is ready to listen."

"Granny," said Gretchen slowly, "it's almost Christmas time, isn't it?"

"Yes, dearie," said Granny, "only five more days now," and then she sighed, but little Gretchen was so happy that she did not notice Granny's sigh.

"What do you think, Granny, I'll get this Christmas?" said she, looking up eagerly into Granny's face.

"Ah, child, child," said Granny, shaking her head, "you'll have no Christmas this year. We are too poor for that."

"Oh, but, Granny," interrupted little Gretchen, "think of all the beautiful toys we saw in the village to-day. Surely Santa Claus has sent enough for every little child."

"Ah, dearie," said Granny, "those toys are for people who can pay money for them, and we have no money to spend for Christmas toys."

"Well, Granny," said Gretchen, "perhaps some of the little children who live in the great house on the hill at the other end of the village will be willing to share some of their toys with me. They will be so glad to give some to a little girl who has none."

"Dear child, dear child," said Granny, leaning forward and stroking the soft, shiny hair of the little girl, "your heart is full of love. You would be glad to bring a Christmas to every child; but their heads are so full of what they are going to get that they forget all about anybody else but themselves." Then she sighed and shook her head.

"Well, Granny," said Gretchen, her bright, happy tone of voice growing a little less joyous, "perhaps the dear Santa Claus will show some of the village children how to make presents that do not cost money, and some of them may surprise me Christmas morning with a present. And, Granny, dear," added she, springing up from her low stool, "can't I gather some of the pine branches and take them to the old sick man who lives in the house by the mill, so that he can have the sweet smell of our pine forest in his room all Christmas day?"

"Yes, dearie," said Granny, "you may do what you can to make the Christmas bright and happy, but you must not expect any present yourself."

"Oh, but, Granny," said little Gretchen, her face brightening, "you forget all about the shining Christmas angels, who came down to earth and sang their wonderful song the night the beautiful Christ-Child was born! They are so loving and good that they will not forget any little child. I shall ask my dear stars to-night to tell them of us. You know," she added, with a look of relief, "the stars are so very high that they must know the angels quite well, as they come and go with their messages from the loving God."

Granny sighed, as she half whispered, "Poor child, poor child!" but Gretchen threw her arm around Granny's neck and gave her a hearty kiss, saying as she did so: "Oh, Granny, Granny, you don't talk to the stars often enough, else you wouldn't be sad at Christmas time." Then she danced all around the room, whirling her little skirts about her to show Granny how the wind had made the snow dance that day. She looked so droll and funny that Granny forgot her cares and worries and laughed with little Gretchen over her new snow-dance. The days passed on, and the morning before Christmas Eve came. Gretchen having tidied up the little room—for Granny had taught her to be a careful little housewife—was off to the forest, singing a birdlike song, almost as happy and free as the birds themselves. She was very busy that day, preparing a surprise for Granny. First, however, she gathered the most beautiful of the fir branches within her reach to take the next morning to the old sick man who lived by the mill. The day was all too short for the happy little girl. When Granny came trudging wearily home that night, she found the frame of the doorway covered with green pine branches.

"It's to welcome you, Granny! It's to welcome you!" cried Gretchen; "our old dear home wanted to give you a Christmas welcome. Don't you see, the branches of evergreen make it look as if it were smiling all over, and it is trying to say, 'A happy Christmas' to you, Granny!"

Granny laughed and kissed the little girl, as they opened the door and went in together. Here was a new surprise for Granny. The four posts of the wooden bed, which stood in one corner of the room, had been trimmed by the busy little fingers, with smaller and more flexible branches of the pine-trees. A small bouquet of red mountain-ash berries stood at each side of the fireplace, and these, together with the trimmed posts of the bed, gave the plain old room quite a festival look. Gretchen laughed and clapped her hands and danced about until the house seemed full of music to poor, tired Granny, whose heart had been sad as she turned toward their home that night, thinking of the disappointment which must come to loving little Gretchen the next morning.

After supper was over little Gretchen drew her stool up to Granny's side, and laying her soft, little hands on Granny's knee, asked to be told once again the story of the coming of the Christ-Child; how the night that he was born the beautiful angels had sung their wonderful song, and how the whole sky had become bright with a strange and glorious light, never seen by the people of earth before. Gretchen had heard the story many, many times before, but she never grew tired of it, and now that Christmas Eve had come again, the happy little child wanted to hear it once more.

When Granny had finished telling it the two sat quiet and silent for a little while thinking it over; then Granny rose and said that it was time for them to go to bed. She slowly took off her heavy wooden shoes, such as are worn in that country, and placed them beside the hearth. Gretchen looked thoughtfully at them for a minute or two, and then she said, "Granny, don't you think that somebody in all this wide world will think of us to-night?"

"Nay, Gretchen," said Granny, "I don't think any one will."

"Well, then, Granny," said Gretchen, "the Christmas angels will, I know; so I am going to take one of your wooden shoes, and put it on the windowsill outside, so that they may see it as they pass by. I am sure the stars will tell the Christmas angels where the shoe is."

"Ah, you foolish, foolish child," said Granny, "you are only getting ready for a disappointment To-morrow morning there will be nothing whatever in the shoe. I can tell you that now."

But little Gretchen would not listen. She only shook her head and cried out: "Ah, Granny, you don't talk enough to the stars." With this she seized the shoe, and, opening the door, hurried out to place it on the windowsill. It was very dark without, and something soft and cold seemed to gently kiss her hair and face. Gretchen knew by this that it was snowing, and she looked up to the sky, anxious to see if the stars were in sight, but a strong wind was tumbling the dark, heavy snow-clouds about and had shut away all else.

"Never mind," said Gretchen softly to herself, "the stars are up there, even if I can't see them, and the Christmas angels do not mind snowstorms."

Just then a rough wind went sweeping by the little girl, whispering something to her which she could not understand, and then it made a sudden rush up to the snow-clouds and parted them, so that the deep, mysterious sky appeared beyond, and shining down out of the midst of it was Gretchen's favourite star.

"Ah, little star, little star!" said the child, laughing aloud, "I knew you were there, though I couldn't see you. Will you whisper to the Christmas angels as they come by that little Gretchen wants so very much to have a Christmas gift to-morrow morning, if they have one to spare, and that she has put one of Granny's shoes upon the windowsill ready for it?"

A moment more and the little girl, standing on tiptoe, had reached the windowsill and placed the shoe upon it, and was back again in the house beside Granny and the warm fire.

The two went quietly to bed, and that night as little Gretchen knelt to pray to the Heavenly Father, she thanked him for having sent the Christ-Child into the world to teach all mankind how to be loving and unselfish, and in a few moments she was quietly sleeping, dreaming of the Christmas angels.

The next morning, very early, even before the sun was up, little Gretchen was awakened by the sound of sweet music coming from the village. She listened for a moment and then she knew that the choir-boys were singing the Christmas carols in the open air of the village street. She sprang up out of bed and began to dress herself as quickly as possible, singing as she dressed. While Granny was slowly putting on her clothes, little Gretchen, having finished dressing herself, unfastened the door and hurried out to see what the Christmas angels had left in the old wooden shoe.

The white snow covered everything—trees, stumps, roads, and pastures—until the whole world looked like fairyland. Gretchen climbed up on a large stone which was beneath the window and carefully lifted down the wooden shoe. The snow tumbled off of it in a shower over the little girl's hands, but she did not heed that; she ran hurriedly back into the house, putting her hand into the toe of the shoe as she ran.

"Oh, Granny! Oh, Granny!" she exclaimed, "you didn't believe the Christmas angels would think about us, but see, they have, they have! Here is a dear little bird nestled down in the toe of your shoe! Oh, isn't he beautiful?"

Granny came forward and looked at what the child was holding lovingly in her hand. There she saw a tiny chick-a-dee, whose wing was evidently broken by the rough and boisterous winds of the night before, and who had taken shelter in the safe, dry toe of the old wooden shoe. She gently took the little bird out of Gretchen's hands, and skilfully bound his broken wing to his side, so that he need not hurt himself by trying to fly with it. Then she showed Gretchen how to make a nice warm nest for the little stranger, close beside the fire, and when their breakfast was ready she let Gretchen feed the little bird with a few moist crumbs.

Later in the day Gretchen carried the fresh, green boughs to the old sick man by the mill, and on her way home stopped to see and enjoy the Christmas toys of some other children whom she knew, never once wishing that they were hers. When she reached home she found that the little bird had gone to sleep. Soon, however, he opened his eyes and stretched his head up, saying just as plain as a bird could say, "Now, my new friends, I want you to give me something more to eat." Gretchen gladly fed him again, and then, holding him in her lap, she softly and gently stroked his gray feathers until the little creature seemed to lose all fear of her. That evening Granny taught her a Christmas hymn and told her another beautiful Christmas story. Then Gretchen made up a funny little story to tell to the birdie. He winked his eyes and turned his head from side to side in such a droll fashion that Gretchen laughed until the tears came.

As Granny and she got ready for bed that night, Gretchen put her arms softly around Granny's neck, and whispered: "What a beautiful Christmas we have had to-day, Granny! Is there anything in the world more lovely than Christmas?"

"Nay, child, nay," said Granny, "not to such loving hearts as yours."

CHRISTMAS GREETINGS FROM A FAIRY TO A CHILD

By Lewis Carroll

Lady dear, if Fairies may
   For a moment lay aside
   Cunning tricks and elfish play,
'Tis at happy Christmas-tide.

We have heard the children say—
Gentle children, whom we love—
Long ago, on Christmas Day,
Came a message from above.

Still, as Christmas-tide comes round,
They remember it again—
Echo still the joyful sound
"Peace on earth, good-will to men!"

Yet the hearts must childlike be
Where such heavenly guests abide:
Unto children, in their glee,
All the year is Christmas-tide!

Thus, forgetting tricks and play
For a moment, Lady dear,
We would wish you, if we may,
Merry Christmas, glad New Year!

THE CHRISTMAS FAIRY OF STRASBURG: A GERMAN FOLK-TALE

By J. Stirling Coyne (Adapted)

Once, long ago, there lived near the ancient city of Strasburg, on the river Rhine, a young and handsome count, whose name was Otto. As the years flew by he remained unwed, and never so much as cast a glance at the fair maidens of the country round; for this reason people began to call him "Stone-Heart."

It chanced that Count Otto, on one Christmas Eve, ordered that a great hunt should take place in the forest surrounding his castle. He and his guests and his many retainers rode forth, and the chase became more and more exciting. It led through thickets, and over pathless tracts of forest, until at length Count Otto found himself separated from his companions.

He rode on by himself until he came to a spring of clear, bubbling water, known to the people around as the "Fairy Well." Here Count Otto dismounted. He bent over the spring and began to lave his hands in the sparkling tide, but to his wonder he found that though the weather was cold and frosty, the water was warm and delightfully caressing. He felt a glow of joy pass through his veins, and, as he plunged his hands deeper, he fancied that his right hand was grasped by another, soft and small, which gently slipped from his finger the gold ring he always wore. And, lo! when he drew out his hand, the gold ring was gone.

Full of wonder at this mysterious event, the count mounted his horse and returned to his castle, resolving in his mind that the very next day he would have the Fairy Well emptied by his servants.

He retired to his room, and, throwing himself just as he was upon his couch, tried to sleep; but the strangeness of the adventure kept him restless and wakeful.

Suddenly he heard the hoarse baying of the watch-hounds in the courtyard, and then the creaking of the drawbridge, as though it were being lowered. Then came to his ear the patter of many small feet on the stone staircase, and next he heard indistinctly the sound of light footsteps in the chamber adjoining his own.

Count Otto sprang from his couch, and as he did so there sounded a strain of delicious music, and the door of his chamber was flung open. Hurrying into the next room, he found himself in the midst of numberless Fairy beings, clad in gay and sparkling robes. They paid no heed to him, but began to dance, and laugh, and sing, to the sound of mysterious music.

In the center of the apartment stood a splendid Christmas Tree, the first ever seen in that country. Instead of toys and candles there hung on its lighted boughs diamond stars, pearl necklaces, bracelets of gold ornamented with colored jewels, aigrettes of rubies and sapphires, silken belts embroidered with Oriental pearls, and daggers mounted in gold and studded with the rarest gems. The whole tree swayed, sparkled, and glittered in the radiance of its many lights.

Count Otto stood speechless, gazing at all this wonder, when suddenly the Fairies stopped dancing and fell back, to make room for a lady of dazzling beauty who came slowly toward him.

She wore on her raven-black tresses a golden diadem set with jewels. Her hair flowed down upon a robe of rosy satin and creamy velvet. She stretched out two small, white hands to the count and addressed him in sweet, alluring tones:—

"Dear Count Otto," said she, "I come to return your Christmas visit. I am Ernestine, the Queen of the Fairies. I bring you something you lost in the Fairy Well."

And as she spoke she drew from her bosom a golden casket, set with diamonds, and placed it in his hands. He opened it eagerly and found within his lost gold ring.

Carried away by the wonder of it all, and overcome by an irresistible impulse, the count pressed the Fairy Ernestine to his heart, while she, holding him by the hand, drew him into the magic mazes of the dance. The mysterious music floated through the room, and the rest of that Fairy company circled and whirled around the Fairy Queen and Count Otto, and then gradually dissolved into a mist of many colors, leaving the count and his beautiful guest alone.

Then the young man, forgetting all his former coldness toward the maidens of the country round about, fell on his knees before the Fairy and besought her to become his bride. At last she consented on the condition that he should never speak the word "death" in her presence.

The next day the wedding of Count Otto and Ernestine, Queen of the Fairies, was celebrated with great pomp and magnificence, and the two continued to live happily for many years.

Now it happened on a time, that the count and his Fairy wife were to hunt in the forest around the castle. The horses were saddled and bridled, and standing at the door, the company waited, and the count paced the hall in great impatience; but still the Fairy Ernestine tarried long in her chamber. At length she appeared at the door of the hall, and the count addressed her in anger.

"You have kept us waiting so long," he cried, "that you would make a good messenger to send for Death!"

Scarcely had he spoken the forbidden and fatal word, when the Fairy, uttering a wild cry, vanished from his sight. In vain Count Otto, overwhelmed with grief and remorse, searched the castle and the Fairy Well, no trace could he find of his beautiful, lost wife but the imprint of her delicate hand set in the stone arch above the castle gate.

Years passed by, and the Fairy Ernestine did not return. The count continued to grieve. Every Christmas Eve he set up a lighted tree in the room where he had first met the Fairy, hoping in vain that she would return to him.

Time passed and the count died. The castle fell into ruins. But to this day may be seen above the massive gate, deeply sunken in the stone arch, the impress of a small and delicate hand.

And such, say the good folk of Strasburg, was the origin of the Christmas Tree.

THE CRATCHITS' CHRISTMAS DINNER
(Adapted)

Charles Dickens

Scrooge and the Ghost of Christmas Present stood in the city streets on Christmas morning, where (for the weather was severe) the people made a rough but brisk and not unpleasant kind of music, in scraping the snow from the pavement in front of their dwellings, and from the tops of their houses, whence it was mad delight to the boys to see it come plumping down into the road below, and splitting into artificial little snowstorms.

The house fronts looked black enough, and the windows blacker, contrasting with the smooth white sheet of snow upon the roofs, and with the dirtier snow upon the ground, which last deposit had been ploughed up in deep furrows by the heavy wheels of carts and wagons; furrows that crossed and recrossed each other hundreds of times where the great streets branched off, and made intricate channels, hard to trace, in the thick yellow mud and icy water. The sky was gloomy, and the shortest streets were choked up with a dingy mist, half thawed, half frozen, whose heavier particles descended in a shower of sooty atoms, as if all the chimneys in Great Britain had, by one consent, caught fire, and were blazing away to their dear heart's content. There was nothing very cheerful in the climate or the town, and yet was there an air of cheerfulness abroad that the dearest summer air and brightest summer sun might have endeavoured to diffuse in vain.

For the people who were shovelling away on the housetops were jovial and full of glee, calling out to one another from the parapets, and now and then exchanging a facetious snowball—better-natured missile far than many a wordy jest—laughing heartily if it went right, and not less heartily if it went wrong. The poulterers' shops were still half open, and the fruiterers' were radiant in their glory. There were great, round, potbellied baskets of chestnuts, shaped like the waistcoats of jolly old gentlemen, lolling at the doors, and tumbling out into the street in their apoplectic opulence.

There were ruddy, brown-faced, broad-girthed Spanish onions, shining in the fatness of their growth like Spanish friars, and winking, from their shelves, in wanton slyness at the girls as they went by, and glanced demurely at the hung-up mistletoe. There were pears and apples, clustering high in blooming pyramids; there were bunches of grapes, made, in the shopkeeper's benevolence, to dangle from conspicuous hooks, that people's mouths might water gratis as they passed; there were piles of filberts, mossy and brown, recalling, in their fragrance, ancient walks among the woods, and pleasant shufflings ankle deep through withered leaves; there were Norfolk biffins, squab and swarthy, setting off the yellow of the oranges and lemons, and, in the great compactness of their juicy persons, urgently entreating and beseeching to be carried home in paper bags and eaten after dinner. The very gold and silver fish, set forth among these choice fruits in a bowl, though members of a dull and stagnant-blooded race, appeared to know that there was something going on; and, to a fish, went gasping round and round their little world in slow and passionless excitement.

The grocers'! oh, the grocers'! nearly closed, with perhaps two shutters down, or one; but through those gaps such glimpses! It was not alone that the scales descending on the counter made a merry sound, or that the twine and roller parted company so briskly, or that the canisters were rattled up and down like juggling tricks, or even that the blended scents of tea and coffee were so grateful to the nose, or even that the raisins were so plentiful and rare, the almonds so extremely white, the sticks of cinnamon so long and straight, the other spices so delicious, the candied fruits so caked and spotted with molten sugar as to make the coldest lookers-on feel faint, and subsequently bilious. Nor was it that the figs were moist and pulpy, or that the French plums blushed in modest tartness from their highly decorated boxes, or that everything was good to eat and in its Christmas dress; but the customers were all so hurried and so eager in the hopeful promise of the day that they tumbled up against each other at the door, crashing their wicker baskets wildly, and left their purchases upon the counter, and came running back to fetch them, and committed hundreds of the like mistakes, in the best humour possible; while the grocer and his people were so frank and fresh that the polished hearts with which they fastened their aprons behind might have been their own, worn outside for general inspection, and for Christmas daws to peck at, if they chose.

But soon the steeples called good people all to church and chapel, and away they came, flocking through the streets in their best clothes, and with their gayest faces. And at the same time there emerged from scores of by-streets, lanes, and nameless turnings, innumerable people, carrying their dinners to the bakers' shops. The sight of these poor revellers appeared to interest the Spirit very much, for he stood, with Scrooge beside him, in a baker's doorway, and, taking off the covers as their bearers passed, sprinkled incense on their dinners from his torch. And it was a very uncommon kind of torch, for once or twice when there were angry words between some dinner-carriers who had jostled each other, he shed a few drops of water on them from it, and their good-humour was restored directly. For they said it was a shame to quarrel upon Christmas Day. And so it was! God love it, so it was!

In time the bells ceased, and the bakers were shut up; and yet there was a genial shadowing forth of all these dinners, and the progress of their cooking, in the thawed blotch of wet above each baker's oven, where the pavement smoked as if its stones were cooking too.

"Is there a peculiar flavour in what you sprinkle from your torch?" asked Scrooge.

"There is. My own."

"Would it apply to any kind of dinner on this day?" asked Scrooge.

"To any kindly given. To a poor one most."

"Why to a poor one most?" asked Scrooge.

"Because it needs it most."

They went on, invisible, as they had been before, into the suburbs of the town. It was a remarkable quality of the Ghost (which Scrooge had observed at the baker's) that, notwithstanding his gigantic size, he could accommodate himself to any place with ease; and that he stood beneath a low roof quite as gracefully, and like a supernatural creature, as it was possible he could have done in any lofty hall.

And perhaps it was the pleasure the good Spirit had in showing off this power of his, or else it was his own kind, generous, hearty nature, and his sympathy with all poor men, that led him straight to Scrooge's clerk's; for there he went, and took Scrooge with him, holding to his robe; and on the threshold of the door the Spirit smiled, and stopped to bless Bob Cratchit's dwelling with the sprinklings of his torch. Think of that! Bob had but fifteen "bob" a week himself; he pocketed on Saturdays but fifteen copies of his Christian name; and yet the Ghost of Christmas Present blessed his four-roomed house!

Then up rose Mrs. Cratchit, Cratchit's wife, dressed out but poorly in a twice-turned gown, but brave in ribbons, which are cheap and make a goodly show for sixpence; and she laid the cloth, assisted by Belinda Cratchit, second of her daughters, also brave in ribbons; while Master Peter Cratchit plunged a fork into the saucepan of potatoes, and getting the corners of his monstrous shirt-collar (Bob's private property, conferred upon his son and heir in honour of the day) into his mouth, rejoiced to find himself so gallantly attired, and yearned to show his linen in the fashionable parks. And now two smaller Cratchits, boy and girl, came tearing in, screaming that outside the baker's they had smelt the goose, and known it for their own, and, basking in luxurious thoughts of sage and onion, these young Cratchits danced about the table, and exalted Master Peter Cratchit to the skies, while he (not proud, although his collar nearly choked him) blew the fire, until the slow potatoes, bubbling up, knocked loudly at the saucepan lid to be let out and peeled.

"What has ever got your precious father, then?" said Mrs. Cratchit. "And your brother, Tiny Tim? And Martha warn't as late last Christmas Day by half an hour!"

"Here's Martha, mother!" said a girl, appearing as she spoke.

"Here's Martha, mother!" cried the two young Cratchits. "Hurrah! There's such a goose, Martha!"

"Why, bless your heart alive, my dear, how late you are!" said Mrs. Cratchit, kissing her a dozen times, and taking off her shawl and bonnet for her with officious zeal.

"We'd a deal of work to finish up last night," replied the girl, "and had to clear away this morning, mother!"

"Well, never mind so long as you are come," said Mrs. Cratchit. "Sit ye down before the fire, my dear, and have a warm, Lord bless ye!"

"No, no! There's father coming!" cried the two young Cratchits, who were everywhere at once.

"Hide, Martha, hide!"

So Martha hid herself, and in came little Bob, the father, with at least three feet of comforter, exclusive of the fringe, hanging down before him, and his threadbare clothes darned up and brushed, to look seasonable; and Tiny Tim upon his shoulder. Alas for Tiny Tim, he bore a little crutch, and had his limbs supported by an iron frame!

"Why, where's our Martha?" cried Bob Cratchit, looking around.

"Not coming," said Mrs. Cratchit.

"Not coming?" said Bob, with a sudden declension in his high spirits; for he had been Tim's blood horse all the way from the church, and had come home rampant. "Not coming upon Christmas Day?"

Martha didn't like to see him disappointed, if it were only in joke; so she came out prematurely from behind the closet door, and ran into his arms, while the two young Cratchits hustled Tiny Tim, and bore him off into the wash-house, that he might hear the pudding singing in the copper.

"And how did little Tim behave?" asked Mrs. Cratchit, when she had rallied Bob on his credulity, and Bob had hugged his daughter to his heart's content.

"As good as gold," said Bob, "and better. Somehow he gets thoughtful, sitting by himself so much, and thinks the strangest things you ever heard. He told me, coming home, that he hoped the people saw him in the church, because he was a cripple, and it might be pleasant to them to remember, upon Christmas Day, who made lame beggars walk, and blind men see."

Bob's voice was tremulous when he told them this, and trembled more when he said that Tiny Tim was growing strong and hearty.

His active little crutch was heard upon the floor, and back came Tiny Tim before another word was spoken, escorted by his brother and sister to his stool beside the fire; and while Bob, turning up his cuffs—as if, poor fellow, they were capable of being made more shabby—compounded some hot mixture in a jug with gin and lemons, and stirred it round and round, and put it on the hob to simmer, Master Peter and the two ubiquitous young

Cratchits went to fetch the goose, with which they soon returned in high procession.

Such a bustle ensued that you might have thought a goose the rarest of all birds—a feathered phenomenon, to which a black swan was a matter of course—and in truth it was something very like it in that house. Mrs. Cratchit made the gravy (ready beforehand in a little saucepan) hissing hot; Master Peter mashed the potatoes with incredible vigour; Miss Belinda sweetened up the apple-sauce; Martha dusted the hot plates; Bob took Tiny Tim beside him in a tiny corner at the table; the two young Cratchits set chairs for everybody, not forgetting themselves, and, mounting guard upon their posts, crammed spoons into their mouths, lest they should shriek for goose before their turn came to be helped. At last the dishes were set on and grace was said. It was succeeded by a breathless pause, as Mrs. Cratchit, looking slowly all along the carving knife, prepared to plunge it into the breast; but when she did, and when the long expected gush of stuffing issued forth, one murmur of delight arose all round the board, and even Tiny Tim, excited by the two young Cratchits, beat on the table with the handle of his knife, and feebly cried, "Hurrah!"

There never was such a goose. Bob said he didn't believe there ever was such a goose cooked. Its tenderness and flavour, size and cheapness, were the themes of universal admiration. Eked out by apple-sauce and mashed potatoes, it was a sufficient dinner for the whole family; indeed, as Mrs. Cratchit said with great delight (surveying one small atom of a bone upon the dish), they hadn't ate it all at last! Yet every one had had enough, and the youngest Cratchits in particular were steeped in sage and onion to the eyebrows! But now, the plates being changed by Miss Belinda,

Mrs. Cratchit left the room alone—too nervous to bear witnesses—to take the pudding up, and bring it in.

Suppose it should not be done enough? Suppose it should break in turning out? Suppose somebody should have got over the wall of the backyard and stolen it, while they were merry with the goose—a supposition at which the two young Cratchits became livid! All sorts of horrors were supposed.

Hallo! A great deal of steam! The pudding was out of the copper. A smell like a washing-day! That was the cloth. A smell like an eating house and a pastry-cook's next door to each other, with a laundress's next door to that! That was the pudding! In half a minute Mrs. Cratchit entered—flushed, but smiling proudly—with the pudding, like a speckled cannon-ball, so hard and firm, blazing in half of half-a-quarter of ignited brandy, and bedight with Christmas holly stuck into the top.

Oh, a wonderful pudding! Bob Cratchit said, and calmly, too, that he regarded it as the greatest success achieved by Mrs. Cratchit since their marriage. Mrs. Cratchit said that, now the weight was off her mind, she would confess she had her doubts about the quantity of flour. Everybody had something to say about it, but nobody thought or said it was at all a small pudding for a large family. It would have been flat heresy to do so. Any Cratchit would have blushed to hint at such a thing.

At last the dinner was all done, the cloth was cleared, the hearth swept, and the fire made up. The compound in the jug being tasted, and considered perfect, tipples and oranges were put upon the table, and a shovelful of chestnuts on the fire. Then all the Cratchit family drew round the hearth in what Bob Cratchit called a circle, meaning half a one; and at Bob Cratchit's elbow stood the family display of glass—two tumblers and a custard-cup without a handle.

These held the hot stuff from the jug, however, as well as golden goblets would have done; and Bob served it out with beaming looks, while the chestnuts on the fire sputtered and cracked noisily. Then Bob proposed:

"A Merry Christmas to us all, my dears. God bless us!"

Which all the family reechoed.

"God bless us every one!" said Tiny Tim, the last of all.

CHRISTMAS AT FEZZIWIG'S WAREHOUSE

By Charles Dickens

"Yo Ho! my boys," said Fezziwig. "No more work tonight! Christmas Eve, Dick! Christmas, Ebenezer! Let's have the shutters up!" cried old Fezziwig with a sharp clap of his hands, "before a man can say Jack Robinson. . "

"Hilli-ho!" cried old Fezziwig, skipping down from the high desk with wonderful agility. "Clear away, my lads, and let's have lots of room here! Hilli-ho, Dick! Cheer-up, Ebenezer!"

Clear away! There was nothing they wouldn't have cleared away, or couldn't have cleared away with old Fezziwig looking on. It was done in a minute. Every movable was packed off, as if it were dismissed from public life forevermore; the floor was swept and watered, the lamps were trimmed, fuel was heaped upon the fire; and the warehouse was as snug, and warm, and dry, and bright a ballroom as you would desire to see on a winter's night.

In came a fiddler with a music book, and went up to the lofty desk and made an orchestra of it and tuned like fifty stomach-aches. In came Mrs. Fezziwig, one vast substantial smile. In came the three Misses Fezziwig, beaming and lovable. In came the six followers whose hearts they broke. In came all the young men and women employed in the business. In came the housemaid with her cousin the baker. In came the cook with her brother's particular friend the milkman. In came the boy from over the way, who was suspected of not having board enough from his master, trying to hide himself behind the girl from next door but one who was proved to have had her ears pulled by her mistress; in they all came, anyhow and everyhow. Away they all went, twenty couple at once; hands half round and back again the other way; down the middle and up again; round and round in various stages of affectionate grouping, old top couple always turning up in the wrong place; new top couple starting off again, as soon as they got there; all top couples at last, and not a bottom one to help them.

When this result was brought about the fiddler struck up "Sir Roger de Coverley." Then old Fezziwig stood out to dance with Mrs. Fezziwig. Top couple, too, with a good stiff piece of work cut out for them; three or four and twenty pairs of partners; people who were not to be trifled with; people who would dance and had no notion of walking.

But if they had been thrice as many--oh, four times as many--old Fezziwig would have been a match for them, and so would Mrs. Fezziwig. As to her, she was worthy to be his partner in every sense of the term. If that's not high praise, tell me higher and I'll use it. A positive light appeared to issue from Fezziwig's calves. They shone in every part of the dance like moons. You couldn't have predicted at any given time what would become of them next. And when old Fezziwig and Mrs. Fezziwig had gone all through the dance, advance and retire; both hands to your partner, bow and courtesy, corkscrew, thread the needle, and back again to your place; Fezziwig "cut"--cut so deftly that he appeared to wink with his legs, and came upon his feet again with a stagger.

When the clock struck eleven the domestic ball broke up. Mr. and Mrs. Fezziwig took their stations, one on either side of the door, and shaking hands with every person individually, as he or she went out, wished him or her a Merry Christmas!

THE GIFT OF THE MAGI

By O. Henry

One dollar and eighty-seven cents. That was all. And sixty cents of it was in pennies. Pennies saved one and two at a time by bulldozing the grocer and the vegetable man and the butcher until one's cheeks burned with the silent imputation of parsimony that such close dealing implied. Three times Della counted it. One dollar and eighty-seven cents. And the next day would be Christmas.

There was clearly nothing to do but flop down on the shabby little couch and howl. So Della did it. Which instigates the moral reflection that life is made up of sobs, sniffles, and smiles, with sniffles predominating.

While the mistress of the home is gradually subsiding from the first stage to the second, take a look at the home. A furnished flat at $8 per week. It did not exactly beggar description, but it certainly had that word on the lookout for the mendicancy squad.

In the vestibule below was a letter-box into which no letter would go, and an electric button from which no mortal finger could coax a ring. Also appertaining thereunto was a card bearing the name "Mr. James Dillingham Young."

The "Dillingham" had been flung to the breeze during a former period of prosperity when its possessor was being paid $30 per week. Now, when the income was shrunk to $20, though, they were thinking seriously of contracting to a modest and unassuming D. But whenever Mr. James Dillingham Young came home and reached his flat above he was called "Jim" and greatly hugged by Mrs. James Dillingham Young, already introduced to you as Della. Which is all very good.

Della finished her cry and attended to her cheeks with the powder rag. She stood by the window and looked out dully at a gray cat walking a gray fence in a gray backyard. Tomorrow would be Christmas Day, and she had only $1.87 with which to buy Jim a present. She had been saving every penny she could for months, with this result. Twenty dollars a week doesn't go far. Expenses had been greater than she had calculated. They always are. Only $1.87 to buy a present for Jim. Her Jim. Many a happy hour she had spent planning for something nice for him. Something fine and rare and sterling—something just a little bit near to being worthy of the honor of being owned by Jim.

There was a pier glass between the windows of the room. Perhaps you have seen a pier glass in an $8 flat. A very thin and very agile person may, by observing his reflection in a rapid sequence of longitudinal strips, obtain a fairly accurate conception of his looks. Della, being slender, had mastered the art.

Suddenly she whirled from the window and stood before the glass. Her eyes were shining brilliantly, but her face had lost its color within twenty seconds. Rapidly she pulled down her hair and let it fall to its full length.

Now, there were two possessions of the James Dillingham Youngs in which they both took a mighty pride. One was Jim's gold watch that had been his father's and his grandfather's. The other was Della's hair. Had the queen of Sheba lived in the flat across the airshaft, Della would have let her hair hang out the window some day to dry just to depreciate Her Majesty's jewels and gifts. Had King Solomon been the janitor, with all his treasures piled up in the basement, Jim would have pulled out his watch every time he passed, just to see him pluck at his beard from envy.

So now Della's beautiful hair fell about her rippling and shining like a cascade of brown waters. It reached below her knee and made itself almost a garment for her. And then she did it up again nervously and quickly. Once she faltered for a minute and stood still while a tear or two splashed on the worn red carpet.

On went her old brown jacket; on went her old brown hat. With a whirl of skirts and with the brilliant sparkle still in her eyes, she fluttered out the door and down the stairs to the street.

Where she stopped the sign read: "Mme. Sofronie. Hair Goods of All Kinds." One flight up Della ran, and collected herself, panting. Madame, large, too white, chilly, hardly looked the "Sofronie."

"Will you buy my hair?" asked Della.

"I buy hair," said Madame. "Take yer hat off and let's have a sight at the looks of it."

Down rippled the brown cascade.

"Twenty dollars," said Madame, lifting the mass with a practised hand.

"Give it to me quick," said Della.

Oh, and the next two hours tripped by on rosy wings. Forget the hashed metaphor. She was ransacking the stores for Jim's present.

She found it at last. It surely had been made for Jim and no one else. There was no other like it in any of the stores, and she had turned all of them inside out. It was a platinum fob chain simple and chaste in design, properly proclaiming its value by substance alone and not by meretricious ornamentation—as all good things should do. It was even worthy of The Watch. As soon as she saw it she knew that it must be Jim's. It was like him. Quietness and value—the description applied to both. Twenty-one dollars they took from her for it, and she hurried home with the 87 cents. With that chain on his watch Jim might be properly anxious about the time in any company. Grand as the watch was, he sometimes looked at it on the sly on account of the old leather strap that he used in place of a chain.

When Della reached home her intoxication gave way a little to prudence and reason. She got out her curling irons and lighted the gas and went to work repairing the ravages made by generosity added to love. Which is always a tremendous task, dear friends—a mammoth task.

Within forty minutes her head was covered with tiny, close-lying curls that made her look wonderfully like a truant schoolboy. She looked at her reflection in the mirror long, carefully, and critically.

"If Jim doesn't kill me," she said to herself, "before he takes a second look at me, he'll say I look like a Coney Island chorus girl. But what could I do—oh! what could I do with a dollar and eighty-seven cents?"

At 7 o'clock the coffee was made and the frying-pan was on the back of the stove hot and ready to cook the chops.

Jim was never late. Della doubled the fob chain in her hand and sat on the corner of the table near the door that he always entered. Then she heard his step on the stair away down on the first flight, and she turned white for just a moment. She had a habit of saying a little silent prayer about the simplest everyday things, and now she whispered: "Please God, make him think I am still pretty."

The door opened and Jim stepped in and closed it. He looked thin and very serious. Poor fellow, he was only twenty-two—and to be burdened with a family! He needed a new overcoat and he was without gloves.

Jim stopped inside the door, as immovable as a setter at the scent of quail. His eyes were fixed upon Della, and there was an expression in them that she could not read, and it terrified her. It was not anger, nor surprise, nor disapproval, nor horror, nor any of the sentiments that she had been prepared for. He simply stared at her fixedly with that peculiar expression on his face.

Della wriggled off the table and went for him.

"Jim, darling," she cried, "don't look at me that way. I had my hair cut off and sold because I couldn't have lived through Christmas without giving you a present. It'll grow out again—you won't mind, will you? I just had to do it. My hair grows awfully fast. Say 'Merry Christmas!' Jim, and let's be happy. You don't know what a nice—what a beautiful, nice gift I've got for you."

"You've cut off your hair?" asked Jim, laboriously, as if he had not arrived at that patent fact yet even after the hardest mental labor.

"Cut it off and sold it," said Della. "Don't you like me just as well, anyhow? I'm me without my hair, ain't I?"

Jim looked about the room curiously.

"You say your hair is gone?" he said, with an air almost of idiocy.

"You needn't look for it," said Della. "It's sold, I tell you—sold and gone, too. It's Christmas Eve, boy. Be good to me, for it went for you. Maybe the hairs of my head were numbered," she went on with sudden serious sweetness, "but nobody could ever count my love for you. Shall I put the chops on, Jim?"

Out of his trance Jim seemed quickly to wake. He enfolded his Della. For ten seconds let us regard with discreet scrutiny some inconsequential object in the other direction. Eight dollars a week or a million a year—what is the difference? A mathematician or a wit would give you the wrong answer. The magi brought valuable gifts, but that was not among them. This dark assertion will be illuminated later on.

Jim drew a package from his overcoat pocket and threw it upon the table.

"Don't make any mistake, Dell," he said, "about me. I don't think there's anything in the way of a haircut or a shave or a shampoo that could make me like my girl any less. But if you'll unwrap that package you may see why you had me going a while at first."

White fingers and nimble tore at the string and paper. And then an ecstatic scream of joy; and then, alas! a quick feminine change to hysterical tears and wails, necessitating the immediate employment of all the comforting powers of the lord of the flat.

For there lay The Combs—the set of combs, side and back, that Della had worshipped long in a Broadway window. Beautiful combs, pure tortoise shell, with jewelled rims—just the shade to wear in the beautiful vanished hair. They were expensive combs, she knew, and her heart had simply craved and yearned over them without the least hope of possession. And now, they were hers, but the tresses that should have adorned the coveted adornments were gone.

But she hugged them to her bosom, and at length she was able to look up with dim eyes and a smile and say: "My hair grows so fast, Jim!"

And then Della leaped up like a little singed cat and cried, "Oh, oh!"

Jim had not yet seen his beautiful present. She held it out to him eagerly upon her open palm. The dull precious metal seemed to flash with a reflection of her bright and ardent spirit.

"Isn't it a dandy, Jim? I hunted all over town to find it. You'll have to look at the time a hundred times a day now. Give me your watch. I want to see how it looks on it."

Instead of obeying, Jim tumbled down on the couch and put his hands under the back of his head and smiled.

"Dell," said he, "let's put our Christmas presents away and keep 'em a while. They're too nice to use just at present. I sold the watch to get the money to buy your combs. And now suppose you put the chops on."

The magi, as you know, were wise men—wonderfully wise men—who brought gifts to the Babe in the manger. They invented the art of giving Christmas presents. Being wise, their gifts were no doubt wise ones, possibly bearing the privilege of exchange in case of duplication. And here I have lamely related to you the uneventful chronicle of two foolish children in a flat who most unwisely sacrificed for each other the greatest treasures of their house. But in a last word to the wise of these days let it be said that of all who give gifts these two were the wisest. Of all who give and receive gifts, such as they are wisest. Everywhere they are wisest. They are the magi.

I HEARD THE BELLS ON CHRISTMAS DAY

By Henry Wadsworth Longfellow

I heard the bells on Christmas Day
   Their old, familiar carols play,
     And wild and sweet
  The words repeat
Of peace on earth, good-will to men!

And thought how, as the day had come,
The belfries of all Christendom
   Had rolled along
   The unbroken song
Of peace on earth, good-will to men!

Till, ringing, singing on its way,
The world revolved from night to day
   A voice, a chime,
   A chant sublime
Of peace on earth, good-will to men!

Then from each black, accursed mouth,
The cannon thundered in the South,
   And with the sound
   The carols drowned
Of peace on earth, good-will to men!

It was as if an earthquake rent
The hearth-stones of a continent,

And made forlorn
   The households born
Of peace on earth, good-will to men!

And in despair I bowed my head ;
"There is no peace on earth," I said ;
   "For hate is strong
   And mocks the song
Of peace on earth, good-will to men!"

Then pealed the bells more loud and deep:
"God is not dead ; nor doth he sleep !
   The Wrong shall fail,
   The Right prevail,
With peace on earth, good-will to men!"

'TWAS THE NIGHT BEFORE CHRISTMAS
A VISIT FROM ST. NICHOLAS

By Clement Clarke Moore

'Twas the night before Christmas,
    when all through the house
    Not a creature was stirring, not even a mouse.
The stockings were hung by the chimney with care,
In hopes that St Nicholas soon would be there.

The children were nestled all snug in their beds,
While visions of sugar-plums danced in their heads.
And mamma in her 'kerchief, and I in my cap,
Had just settled our brains for a long winter's nap.

When out on the lawn there arose such a clatter,
I sprang from the bed to see what was the matter.
Away to the window I flew like a flash,
Tore open the shutters and threw up the sash.

The moon on the breast of the new-fallen snow
Gave the lustre of mid-day to objects below.
When, what to my wondering eyes should appear,
But a miniature sleigh, and eight tiny reindeer.

With a little old driver, so lively and quick,
I knew in a moment it must be St Nick.
More rapid than eagles his coursers they came,
And he whistled, and shouted, and called them by name!

"Now Dasher! now, Dancer! now, Prancer and Vixen!
On, Comet! On, Cupid! on, on Donner and Blitzen!
To the top of the porch! to the top of the wall!
Now dash away! Dash away! Dash away all!"

As dry leaves that before the wild hurricane fly,
When they meet with an obstacle, mount to the sky.
So up to the house-top the coursers they flew,
With the sleigh full of Toys, and St Nicholas too.

And then, in a twinkling, I heard on the roof
The prancing and pawing of each little hoof.
As I drew in my head, and was turning around,
Down the chimney St Nicholas came with a bound.

He was dressed all in fur, from his head to his foot,
And his clothes were all tarnished with ashes and soot.
A bundle of Toys he had flung on his back,
And he looked like a peddler, just opening his pack.

His eyes-how they twinkled! his dimples how merry!
His cheeks were like roses, his nose like a cherry!
His droll little mouth was drawn up like a bow,
And the beard of his chin was as white as the snow.

The stump of a pipe he held tight in his teeth,
And the smoke it encircled his head like a wreath.
He had a broad face and a little round belly,
That shook when he laughed, like a bowlful of jelly!

He was chubby and plump, a right jolly old elf,
And I laughed when I saw him, in spite of myself!
A wink of his eye and a twist of his head,
Soon gave me to know I had nothing to dread.

He spoke not a word, but went straight to his work,
And filled all the stockings, then turned with a jerk.
And laying his finger aside of his nose,
And giving a nod, up the chimney he rose!

He sprang to his sleigh, to his team gave a whistle,
And away they all flew like the down of a thistle.
But I heard him exclaim, 'ere he drove out of sight,
"Happy Christmas to all, and to all a good-night!"

THE END

A CHRISTMAS FAIRY

John Strange Winter

It was getting very near to Christmas time, and all the boys at Miss Ware's school were talking about going home for the holidays.

"I shall go to the Christmas festival," said Bertie Fellows, "and my mother will have a party, and my Aunt will give another. Oh! I shall have a splendid time at home."

"My Uncle Bob is going to give me a pair of skates," remarked Harry Wadham.

"My father is going to give me a bicycle," put in George Alderson.

"Will you bring it back to school with you?" asked Harry.

"Oh! yes, if Miss Ware doesn't say no."

"Well, Tom," cried Bertie, "where are you going to spend your holidays?"

"I am going to stay here," answered Tom in a very forlorn voice.

"Here—at school—oh, dear! Why can't you go home?"

"I can't go home to India," answered Tom.

"Nobody said you could. But haven't you any relatives anywhere?"

Tom shook his head. "Only in India," he said sadly.

"Poor fellow! That's hard luck for you. I'll tell you what it is, boys, if I couldn't go home for the holidays, especially at Christmas—I think I would just sit down and die."

"Oh, no, you wouldn't," said Tom. "You would get ever so homesick, but you wouldn't die. You would just get through somehow, and hope something would happen before next year, or that some kind fairy would—"

"There are no fairies nowadays," said Bertie.

"See here, Tom, I'll write and ask my mother to invite you to go home with me for the holidays."

"Will you really?"

"Yes, I will. And if she says yes, we shall have such a splendid time. We live in London, you know, and have lots of parties and fun."

"Perhaps she will say no?" suggested poor little Tom.

"My mother isn't the kind that says no," Bertie declared loudly.

In a few days' time a letter arrived from Bertie's mother. The boy opened it eagerly. It said:

My own dear Bertie:

I am very sorry to tell you that little Alice is ill with scarlet fever. And so you cannot come for your holidays. I would have been glad to have you bring your little friend with you if all had been well here.

Your father and I have decided that the best thing that you can do is to stay at Miss Ware's. We shall send your Christmas present to you as well as we can.

It will not be like coming home, but I am sure you will try to be happy, and make me feel that you are helping me in this sad time.

Dear little Alice is very ill, very ill indeed. Tell Tom that I am sending you a box for both of you, with two of everything. And tell him that it makes me so much happier to know that you will not be alone.

Your own mother.

When Bertie Fellows received this letter, which ended all his Christmas hopes and joys, he hid his face upon his desk and sobbed aloud. The lonely boy from India, who sat next to him, tried to comfort his friend in every way he could think of. He patted his shoulder and whispered many kind words to him.

At last Bertie put the letter into Tom's hands. "Read it," he sobbed.

So then Tom understood the cause of Bertie's grief. "Don't fret over it," he said at last. "It might be worse. Why, your father and mother might be thousands of miles away, like mine are. When Alice is better, you will be able to go home. And it will help your mother if she thinks you are almost as happy as if you could go now."

Soon Miss Ware came to tell Bertie how sorry she was for him.

"After all," said she, smiling down on the two boys, "it is an ill wind that blows nobody good. Poor Tom has been expecting to spend his holidays alone, and now he will have a friend with him—Try to look on the bright side, Bertie, and to remember how much worse it would have been if there had been no boy to stay with you."

"I can't help being disappointed, Miss Ware," said Bertie, his eyes filling with tears.

"No; you would be a strange boy if you were not. But I want you to try to think of your poor mother, and write her as cheerfully as you can."

"Yes," answered Bertie; but his heart was too full to say more.

The last day of the term came, and one by one, or two by two, the boys went away, until only Bertie and Tom were left in the great house. It had never seemed so large to either of them before.

"It's miserable," groaned poor Bertie, as they strolled into the schoolroom. "Just think if we were on our way home now—how different."

"Just think if I had been left here by myself," said Tom.

"Yes," said Bertie, "but you know when one wants to go home he never thinks of the boys that have no home to go to."

The evening passed, and the two boys went to bed. They told stories to each other for a long time before they could go to sleep. That night they dreamed of their homes, and felt very lonely. Yet each tried to be brave, and so another day began.

This was the day before Christmas. Quite early in the morning came the great box of which Bertie's mother had spoken in her letter. Then, just as dinner had come to an end, there was a peal of the bell, and a voice was heard asking for Tom Egerton.

Tom sprang to his feet, and flew to greet a tall, handsome lady, crying, "Aunt Laura! Aunt Laura!"

And Laura explained that she and her husband had arrived in London only the day before. "I was so afraid, Tom," she said, "that we should not get here until Christmas Day was over and that you would be disappointed. So I would not let your mother write you that we were on our way home. You must get your things packed up at once, and go back with me to London. Then uncle and I will give you a splendid time."

For a minute or two Tom's face shone with delight. Then he caught sight of Bertie and turned to his aunt.

"Dear Aunt Laura," he said, "I am very sorry, but I can't go."

"Can't go? and why not?"

"Because I can't go and leave Bertie here all alone," he said stoutly. "When I was going to be alone he wrote and asked his mother to let me go home with him. She could not have either of us because Bertie's sister has scarlet fever. He has to stay here, and he has never been away from home at Christmas time before, and I can't go away and leave him by himself, Aunt Laura."

For a minute Aunt Laura looked at the boy as if she could not believe him. Then she caught him in her arms and kissed him.

"You dear little boy, you shall not leave him. You shall bring him along, and we shall all enjoy ourselves together. Bertie, my boy, you are not very old yet, but I am going to teach you a lesson as well as I can. It is that kindness is never wasted in this world."

And so Bertie and Tom found that there was such a thing as a fairy after all.

CHRISTMAS; OR, THE GOOD FAIRY

By Harriet Beecher Stowe

"O, dear! Christmas is coming in a fortnight, and I have got to think up presents for every body!" said young Ellen Stuart, as she leaned languidly back in her chair. "Dear me, it's so tedious! Every body has got every thing that can be thought of."

"O, no," said her confidential adviser, Miss Lester, in a soothing tone. "You have means of buying every thing you can fancy; and when every shop and store is glittering with all manner of splendors, you cannot surely be at a loss."

"Well, now, just listen. To begin with, there's mamma. What can I get for her? I have thought of ever so many things. She has three card cases, four gold thimbles, two or three gold chains, two writing desks of different patterns; and then as to rings, brooches, boxes, and all other things, I should think she might be sick of the sight of them. I am sure I am," said she, languidly gazing on her white and jewelled fingers.

This view of the case seemed rather puzzling to the adviser, and there was silence for a few moments, when Ellen, yawning, resumed:--

"And then there's Cousins Jane and Mary; I suppose they will be coming down on me with a whole load of presents; and Mrs. B. will send me something--she did last year; and then there's Cousins William and Tom--I must get them something; and I would like to do it well enough, if I only knew what to get."

"Well," said Eleanor's aunt, who had been sitting quietly rattling her knitting needles during this speech, "it's a pity that you had not such a subject to practise on as I was when I was a girl. Presents did not fly about in those days as they do now. I remember, when I was ten years old, my father gave me a most marvellously ugly sugar dog for a Christmas gift, and I was perfectly delighted with it, the very idea of a present was so new to us."

"Dear aunt, how delighted I should be if I had any such fresh, unsophisticated body to get presents for! But to get and get for people that have more than they know what to do with now; to add pictures, books, and gilding when the centre tables are loaded with them now, and rings and jewels when they are a perfect drug! I wish myself that I were not sick, and sated, and tired with having every thing in the world given me."

"Well, Eleanor," said her aunt, "if you really do want unsophisticated subjects to practise on, I can put you in the way of it. I can show you more than one family to whom you might seem to be a very good fairy, and where such gifts as you could give with all ease would seem like a magic dream."

"Why, that would really be worth while, aunt."

"Look over in that back alley," said her aunt. "You see those buildings?"

"That miserable row of shanties? Yes."

"Well, I have several acquaintances there who have never been tired of Christmas gifts, or gifts of any other kind. I assure you, you could make quite a sensation over there."

"Well, who is there? Let us know."

"Do you remember Owen, that used to make your shoes?"

"Yes, I remember something about him."

"Well, he has fallen into a consumption, and cannot work any more; and he, and his wife, and three little children live in one of the rooms."

"How do they get along?"

"His wife takes in sewing sometimes, and sometimes goes out washing. Poor Owen! I was over there yesterday; he looks thin and wasted, and his wife was saying that he was parched with constant fever, and had very little appetite. She had, with great self-denial, and by restricting herself almost of necessary food, got him two or three oranges; and the poor fellow seemed so eager after them!"

"Poor fellow!" said Eleanor, involuntarily.

"Now," said her aunt, "suppose Owen's wife should get up on Christmas morning and find at the door a couple of dozen of oranges, and some of those nice white grapes, such as you had at your party last week; don't you think it would make a sensation?"

"Why, yes, I think very likely it might; but who else, aunt? You spoke of a great many."

"Well, on the lower floor there is a neat little room, that is always kept perfectly trim and tidy; it belongs to a young couple who have nothing beyond the husband's day wages to live on. They are, nevertheless, as cheerful and chipper as a couple of wrens; and she is up and down half a dozen times a day, to help poor Mrs. Owen. She has a baby of her own, about five months old, and of course does all the cooking, washing, and ironing for herself and husband; and yet, when Mrs. Owen goes out to wash, she takes her baby, and keeps it whole days for her."

"I'm sure she deserves that the good fairies should smile on her," said Eleanor; "one baby exhausts my stock of virtues very rapidly."

"But you ought to see her baby," said Aunt E.; "so plump, so rosy, and good-natured, and always clean as a lily. This baby is a sort of household shrine; nothing is too sacred or too good for it; and I believe the little thrifty woman feels only one temptation to be extravagant, and that is to get some ornaments to adorn this little divinity."

"Why, did she ever tell you so?"

"No; but one day, when I was coming down stairs, the door of their room was partly open, and I saw a pedler there with open box. John, the husband, was standing with a little purple cap on his hand, which he was regarding with mystified, admiring air, as if he didn't quite comprehend it, and trim little Mary gazing at it with longing eyes.

"'I think we might get it,' said John.

"'O, no,' said she, regretfully; 'yet I wish we could, it's so pretty!'"

"Say no more, aunt. I see the good fairy must pop a cap into the window on Christmas morning. Indeed, it shall be done. How they will wonder where it came from, and talk about it for months to come!"

"Well, then," continued her aunt, "in the next street to ours there is a miserable building, that looks as if it were just going to topple over; and away up in the third story, in a little room just under the eaves, live two poor, lonely old women. They are both nearly on to ninety. I was in there day before yesterday. One of them is constantly confined to her bed with rheumatism; the other, weak and feeble, with failing sight and trembling hands, totters about, her only helper; and they are entirely dependent on charity."

"Can't they do any thing? Can't they knit?" said Eleanor.

"You are young and strong, Eleanor, and have quick eyes and nimble fingers; how long would it take you to knit a pair of stockings?"

"I?" said Eleanor. "What an idea! I never tried, but I think I could get a pair done in a week, perhaps."

"And if somebody gave you twenty-five cents for them, and out of this you had to get food, and pay room rent, and buy coal for your fire, and oil for your lamp----"

"Stop, aunt, for pity's sake!"

"Well, I will stop; but they can't: they must pay so much every month for that miserable shell they live in, or be turned into the street. The meal and flour that some kind person sends goes off for them just as it does for others, and they must get more or starve; and coal is now scarce and high priced."

"O aunt, I'm quite convinced, I'm sure; don't run me down and annihilate me with all these terrible realities. What shall I do to play good fairy to these poor old women?"

"If you will give me full power, Eleanor, I will put up a basket to be sent to them that will give them something to remember all winter."

"O, certainly I will. Let me see if I can't think of something myself."

"Well, Eleanor, suppose, then, some fifty or sixty years hence, if you were old, and your father, and mother, and aunts, and uncles, now so thick around you, lay cold and silent in so many graves--you have somehow got away off to a strange city, where you were never known--you live in a miserable garret, where snow blows at night through the cracks, and the fire is very apt to go out in the old cracked stove--you sit crouching over the dying embers the evening before Christmas--nobody to speak to you, nobody to care for you, except another poor old soul who lies moaning in the bed. Now, what would you like to have sent you?"

"O aunt, what a dismal picture!"

"And yet, Ella, all poor, forsaken old women are made of young girls, who expected it in their youth as little as you do, perhaps."

"Say no more, aunt. I'll buy--let me see--a comfortable warm shawl for each of these poor women; and I'll send them--let me see--O, some tea--nothing goes down with old women like tea; and I'll make John wheel some coal over to them; and, aunt, it would not be a very bad thought to send them a new stove. I remember, the other day, when mamma was pricing stoves, I saw some such nice ones for two or three dollars."

"For a new hand, Ella, you work up the idea very well," said her aunt.

"But how much ought I to give, for any one case, to these women, say?"

"How much did you give last year for any single Christmas present?"

"Why, six or seven dollars for some; those elegant souvenirs were seven dollars; that ring I gave Mrs. B. was twenty."

"And do you suppose Mrs. B. was any happier for it?"

"No, really, I don't think she cared much about it; but I had to give her something, because she had sent me something the year before, and I did not want to send a paltry present to one in her circumstances."

"Then, Ella, give the same to any poor, distressed, suffering creature who really needs it, and see in how many forms of good such a sum will appear. That one hard, cold, glittering ring, that now cheers nobody, and means nothing, that you give because you must, and she takes because she must, might, if broken up into smaller sums, send real warm and heartfelt gladness through many a cold and cheerless dwelling, through many an aching heart."

"You are getting to be an orator, aunt; but don't you approve of Christmas presents, among friends and equals?"

"Yes, indeed," said her aunt, fondly stroking her head. "I have had some Christmas presents that did me a world of good--a little book mark, for instance, that a certain niece of mine worked for me, with wonderful secrecy, three years ago, when she was not a young lady with a purse full of money--that book mark was a true Christmas present; and my young couple across the way are plotting a profound surprise to each other on Christmas morning. John has contrived, by an hour of extra work every night, to lay by enough to get Mary a new calico dress; and she, poor soul, has bargained away the only thing in the jewelry line she ever possessed, to be laid out on a new hat for him.

"I know, too, a washerwoman who has a poor, lame boy--a patient, gentle little fellow--who has lain quietly for weeks and months in his little crib, and his mother is going to give him a splendid Christmas present."

"What is it, pray?"

"A whole orange! Don't laugh. She will pay ten whole cents for it; for it shall be none of your common oranges, but a picked one of the very best going! She has put by the money, a cent at a time, for a whole month; and nobody knows which will be happiest in it, Willie or his mother. These are such Christmas presents as I like to think of--gifts coming from love, and tending to produce love; these are the appropriate gifts of the day."

"But don't you think that it's right for those who have money to give expensive presents, supposing always, as you say, they are given from real affection?"

"Sometimes, undoubtedly. The Savior did not condemn her who broke an alabaster box of ointment--very precious--simply as a proof of love, even although the suggestion was made, 'This might have been sold for three hundred pence, and given to the poor.' I have thought he would regard with sympathy the fond efforts which human love sometimes makes to express itself by gifts, the rarest and most costly. How I rejoiced with all my heart, when Charles Elton gave his poor mother that splendid Chinese shawl and gold watch! because I knew they came from the very fulness of his heart to a mother that he could not do too much for- -a mother that has done and suffered every thing for him. In some such cases, when resources are ample, a costly gift seems to have a graceful appropriateness; but I cannot approve of it if it exhausts all the means of doing for the poor; it is better, then, to give a simple offering, and to do something for those who really need it."

Eleanor looked thoughtful; her aunt laid down her knitting, and said,

in a tone of gentle seriousness, "Whose birth does Christmas commemorate, Ella?"

"Our Savior's, certainly, aunt."

"Yes," said her aunt. "And when and how was he born? In a stable! laid in a manger; thus born, that in all ages he might be known as the brother and friend of the poor. And surely, it seems but appropriate to commemorate his birthday by an especial remembrance of the lowly, the poor, the outcast, and distressed; and if Christ should come back to our city on a Christmas day, where should we think it most appropriate to his character to find him? Would he be carrying splendid gifts to splendid dwellings, or would he be gliding about in the cheerless haunts of the desolate, the poor, the forsaken, and the sorrowful?"

And here the conversation ended.

* * * * *

"What sort of Christmas presents is Ella buying?" said Cousin Tom, as the waiter handed in a portentous-looking package, which had been just rung in at the door.

"Let's open it," said saucy Will. "Upon my word, two great gray blanket shawls! These must be for you and me, Tom! And what's this? A great bolt of cotton flannel and gray yarn stockings!"

The door bell rang again, and the waiter brought in another bulky parcel, and deposited it on the marble-topped centre table.

"What's here?" said Will, cutting the cord. "Whew! a perfect nest of packages! oolong tea! oranges! grapes! white sugar! Bless me, Ella must be going to housekeeping!"

"Or going crazy!" said Tom; "and on my word," said he, looking out of the window, "there's a drayman ringing at our door, with a stove, with a teakettle set in the top of it!"

"Ella's cook stove, of course," said Will; and just at this moment the young lady entered, with her purse hanging gracefully over her hand.

"Now, boys, you are too bad!" she exclaimed, as each of the mischievous youngsters were gravely marching up and down, attired in a gray shawl.

"Didn't you get them for us? We thought you did," said both.

"Ella, I want some of that cotton flannel, to make me a pair of pantaloons," said Tom.

"I say, Ella," said Will, "when are you going to housekeeping? Your cooking stove is standing down in the street; 'pon my word, John is loading some coal on the dray with it."

"Ella, isn't that going to be sent to my office?" said Tom; "do you know I do so languish for a new stove with a teakettle in the top, to heat a fellow's shaving water!"

Just then, another ring at the door, and the grinning waiter handed in a small brown paper parcel for Miss Ella. Tom made a dive at it, and staving off the brown paper, developed a jaunty little purple velvet cap, with silver tassels.

"My smoking cap, as I live!" said he; "only I shall have to wear it on my thumb, instead of my head--too small entirely," said he, shaking his head gravely.

"Come, you saucy boys," said Aunt E., entering briskly, "what are you teasing Ella for?"

"Why, do see this lot of things, aunt! What in the world is Ella going to do with them?"

"O, I know!"

"You know! Then I can guess, aunt, it is some of your charitable works. You are going to make a juvenile Lady Bountiful of El, eh?"

Ella, who had colored to the roots of her hair at the expose of her very unfashionable Christmas preparations, now took heart, and bestowed a very gentle and salutary little cuff on the saucy head that still wore the purple cap, and then hastened to gather up her various purchases.

"Laugh away," said she, gayly; "and a good many others will laugh, too, over these things. I got them to make people laugh--people that are not in the habit of laughing!"

"Well, well, I see into it," said Will; "and I tell you I think right well of the idea, too. There are worlds of money wasted, at this time of the year, in getting things that nobody wants, and nobody cares for after they are got; and I am glad, for my part, that you are going to get up a variety in this line; in fact, I should like to give you one of these stray leaves to help on," said he, dropping a ten dollar note into her paper. "I like to encourage girls to think of something besides breastpins and sugar candy."

But our story spins on too long. If any body wants to see the results of Ella's first attempts at good fairyism, they can call at the doors of two or three old buildings on Christmas morning, and they shall hear all about it.

THE ELVES AND THE SHOEMAKER

By The Brothers Grimm

There was once a shoemaker, who worked very hard and was very honest: but still he could not earn enough to live upon; and at last all he had in the world was gone, save just leather enough to make one pair of shoes.

Then he cut his leather out, all ready to make up the next day, meaning to rise early in the morning to his work. His conscience was clear and his heart light amidst all his troubles; so he went peaceably to bed, left all his cares to Heaven, and soon fell asleep. In the morning after he had said his prayers, he sat himself down to his work; when, to his great wonder, there stood the shoes all ready made, upon the table. The good man knew not what to say or think at such an odd thing happening. He looked at the workmanship; there was not one false stitch in the whole job; all was so neat and true, that it was quite a masterpiece.

The same day a customer came in, and the shoes suited him so well that he willingly paid a price higher than usual for them; and the poor shoemaker, with the money, bought leather enough to make two pairs more. In the evening he cut out the work, and went to bed early, that he might get up and begin betimes next day; but he was saved all the trouble, for when he got up in the morning the work was done ready to his hand. Soon in came buyers, who paid him handsomely for his goods, so that he bought leather enough for four pair more. He cut out the work again overnight and found it done in the morning, as before; and so it went on for some time: what was got ready in the evening was always done by daybreak, and the good man soon became thriving and well off again.

One evening, about Christmas-time, as he and his wife were sitting over the fire chatting together, he said to her, 'I should like to sit up and watch tonight, that we may see who it is that comes and does my work for me.' The wife liked the thought; so they left a light burning, and hid themselves in a corner of the room, behind a curtain that was hung up there, and watched what would happen.

As soon as it was midnight, there came in two little naked dwarfs; and they sat themselves upon the shoemaker's bench, took up all the work that was cut out, and began to ply with their little fingers, stitching and rapping and tapping away at such a rate, that the shoemaker was all wonder, and could not take his eyes off them. And on they went, till the job was quite done, and the shoes stood ready for use upon the table. This was long before daybreak; and then they bustled away as quick as lightning.

The next day the wife said to the shoemaker. 'These little wights have made us rich, and we ought to be thankful to them, and do them a good turn if we can. I am quite sorry to see them run about as they do; and indeed it is not very decent, for they have nothing upon their backs to keep off the cold. I'll tell you what, I will make each of them a shirt, and a coat and waistcoat, and a pair of pantaloons into the bargain; and do you make each of them a little pair of shoes.'

The thought pleased the good cobbler very much; and one evening, when all the things were ready, they laid them on the table, instead of the work that they used to cut out, and then went and hid themselves, to watch what the little elves would do.

About midnight in they came, dancing and skipping, hopped round the room, and then went to sit down to their work as usual; but when they saw the clothes lying for them, they laughed and chuckled, and seemed mightily delighted.

Then they dressed themselves in the twinkling of an eye, and danced and capered and sprang about, as merry as could be; till at last they danced out at the door, and away over the green.

The good couple saw them no more; but everything went well with them from that time forward, as long as they lived.

PAPA PANOV'S SPECIAL CHRISTMAS

By Leo Tolstoy

It was Christmas Eve and although it was still afternoon, lights had begun to appear in the shops and houses of the little Russian village, for the short winter day was nearly over. Excited children scurried indoors and now only muffled sounds of chatter and laughter escaped from closed shutters.

Old Papa Panov, the village shoemaker, stepped outside his shop to take one last look around. The sounds of happiness, the bright lights and the faint but delicious smells of Christmas cooking reminded him of past Christmas times when his wife had still been alive and his own children little. Now they had gone. His usually cheerful face, with the little laughter wrinkles behind the round steel spectacles, looked sad now. But he went back indoors with a firm step, put up the shutters and set a pot of coffee to heat on the charcoal stove. Then, with a sigh, he settled in his big armchair.

Papa Panov did not often read, but tonight he pulled down the big old family Bible and, slowly tracing the lines with one forefinger, he read again the Christmas story. He read how Mary and Joseph, tired by their journey to Bethlehem, found no room for them at the inn, so that Mary's little baby was born in the cowshed.

"Oh, dear, oh, dear!" exclaimed Papa Panov, "if only they had come here! I would have given them my bed and I could have covered the baby with my patchwork quilt to keep him warm."

He read on about the wise men who had come to see the baby Jesus, bringing him splendid gifts. Papa Panov's face fell. "I have no gift that I could give him," he thought sadly.

Then his face brightened. He put down the Bible, got up and stretched his long arms to the shelf high up in his little room. He took down a small, dusty box and opened it. Inside was a perfect pair of tiny leather shoes. Papa Panov smiled with satisfaction. Yes, they were as good as he had remembered -- the best shoes he had ever made. "I should give him those," he decided, as he gently put them away and sat down again.

He was feeling tired now, and the further he read the sleepier he became. The print began to dance before his eyes so that he closed them, just for a minute. In no time at all Papa Panov was fast asleep.

And as he slept he dreamed. He dreamed that someone was in his room and he knew at once, as one does in dreams, who the person was. It was Jesus.

"You have been wishing that you could see me, Papa Panov." he said kindly, "then look for me tomorrow. It will be Christmas Day and I will visit you. But look carefully, for I shall not tell you who I am."

When at last Papa Panov awoke, the bells were ringing out and a thin light was filtering through the shutters. "Bless my soul!" said Papa Panov. "It's Christmas Day!"

He stood up and stretched himself for he was rather stiff. Then his face filled with happiness as he remembered his dream. This would be a very special Christmas after all, for Jesus was coming to visit him. How would he look? Would he be a little baby, as at that first Christmas? Would he be a grown man, a carpenter -- or the great King that he is, God's Son? He must watch carefully the whole day through so that he recognized him however he came.

Papa Panov put on a special pot of coffee for his Christmas breakfast, took down the shutters and looked out of the window. The street was deserted, no one was stirring yet. No one except the road sweeper. He looked as miserable and dirty as ever, and well he might! Whoever wanted to work on Christmas Day -- and in the raw cold and bitter freezing mist of such a morning?

Papa Panov opened the shop door, letting in a thin stream of cold air. "Come in!" he shouted across the street cheerily. "Come in and have some hot coffee to keep out the cold!"

The sweeper looked up, scarcely able to believe his ears. He was only too glad to put down his broom and come into the warm room. His old clothes steamed gently in the heat of the stove and he clasped both red hands round the comforting warm mug as he drank.

Papa Panov watched him with satisfaction, but every now and them his eyes strayed to the window. It would never do to miss his special visitor.

"Expecting someone?" the sweeper asked at last. So Papa Panov told him about his dream.

"Well, I hope he comes," the sweeper said, "you've given me a bit of Christmas cheer I never expected to have. I'd say you deserve to have your dream come true." And he actually smiled.

When he had gone, Papa Panov put on cabbage soup for his dinner, then went to the door again, scanning the street. He saw no one. But he was mistaken. Someone was coming.

The girl walked so slowly and quietly, hugging the walls of shops and houses, that it was a while before he noticed her. She looked very tired and she was carrying something. As she drew nearer he could see that it was a baby, wrapped in a thin shawl. There was such sadness in her face and in the pinched little face of the baby, that Papa Panov's heart went out to them.

"Won't you come in," he called, stepping outside to meet them. "You both need a warm seat by the fire and a rest."

The young mother let him shepherd her indoors and to the comfort of the armchair. She gave a big sigh of relief.

"I'll warm some milk for the baby," Papa Panov said, "I've had children of my own -- I can feed her for you." He took the milk from the stove and carefully fed the baby from a spoon, warming her tiny feet by the stove at the same time.

"She needs shoes," the cobbler said.

But the girl replied, "I can't afford shoes, I've got no husband to bring home money. I'm on my way to the next village to get work."

A sudden thought flashed through Papa Panov's mind. He remembered the little shoes he had looked at last night. But he had been keeping those for Jesus. He looked again at the cold little feet and made up his mind.

"Try these on her," he said, handing the baby and the shoes to the mother. The beautiful little shoes were a perfect fit. The girl smiled happily and the baby gurgled with pleasure.

"You have been so kind to us," the girl said, when she got up with her baby to go. "May all your Christmas wishes come true!"

But Papa Panov was beginning to wonder if his very special Christmas wish would come true. Perhaps he had missed his visitor? He looked anxiously up and down the street. There were plenty of people about but they were all faces that he recognized. There were neighbors going to call on their families. They nodded and smiled and wished him Happy Christmas! Or beggars -- and Papa Panov hurried indoors to fetch them hot soup and a generous hunk of bread, hurrying out again in case he missed the Important Stranger.

All too soon the winter dusk fell. When Papa Panov next went to the door and strained his eyes, he could no longer make out the passers-by. Most were home and indoors by now anyway. He walked slowly back into his room at last, put up the shutters, and sat down wearily in his armchair.

So it had been just a dream after all. Jesus had not come.

Then all at once he knew that he was no longer alone in the room.

This was not dream for he was wide awake. At first he seemed to see before his eyes the long stream of people who had come to him that day. He saw again the old road sweeper, the young mother and her baby and the beggars he had fed. As they passed, each whispered, "Didn't you see me, Papa Panov?"

"Who are you?" he called out, bewildered.

Then another voice answered him. It was the voice from his dream -- the voice of Jesus.

"I was hungry and you fed me," he said. "I was naked and you clothed me. I was cold and you warmed me. I came to you today in everyone of those you helped and welcomed."

Then all was quiet and still. Only the sound of the big clock ticking. A great peace and happiness seemed to fill the room, overflowing Papa Panov's heart until he wanted to burst out singing and laughing and dancing with joy.

"So he did come after all!" was all that he said.

CHRISTMAS IN SEVENTEEN SEVENTY-SIX

By Anne Hollingsworth Wharton

"On Christmas day in Seventy-six,
   Our gallant troops with bayonets fixed,
   To Trenton marched away."

Children, have any of you ever thought of what little people like you were doing in this country more than a hundred years ago, when the cruel tide of war swept over its bosom? From many homes the fathers were absent, fighting bravely for the liberty which we now enjoy, while the mothers no less valiantly struggled against hardships and discomforts in order to keep a home for their children, whom you only know as your great-grandfathers and great-grandmothers, dignified gentlemen and beautiful ladies, whose painted portraits hang upon the walls in some of your homes. Merry, romping children they were in those far-off times, yet their bright faces must have looked grave sometimes, when they heard the grown people talk of the great things that were happening around them. Some of these little people never forgot the wonderful events of which they heard, and afterward related them to their children and grandchildren, which accounts for some of the interesting stories which you may still hear, if you are good children.

The Christmas story that I have to tell you is about a boy and girl who lived in Bordentown, New Jersey. The father of these children was a soldier in General Washington's army, which was encamped a few miles north of Trenton, on the Pennsylvania side of the Delaware River. Bordentown, as you can see by looking on your map, if you have not hidden them all away for the holidays, is about seven miles south of Trenton, where fifteen hundred Hessians and a troop of British light horse were holding the town. Thus you see that the British, in force, were between Washington's army and Bordentown, besides which there were some British and Hessian troops in the very town. All this seriously interfered with Captain Tracy's going home to eat his Christmas dinner with his wife and children. Kitty and Harry Tracy, who had not lived long enough to see many wars, could not imagine such a thing as Christmas without their father, and had busied themselves for weeks in making everything ready to have a merry time with him. Kitty, who loved to play quite as much as any frolicsome Kitty of to-day, had spent all her spare time in knitting a pair of thick woollen stockings, which seems a wonderful feat for a little girl only eight years old to perform! Can you not see her sitting by the great chimney-place, filled with its roaring, crackling logs, in her quaint, short-waisted dress, knitting away steadily, and puckering up her rosy, dimpled face over the strange twists and turns of that old stocking? I can see her, and I can also hear her sweet voice as she chatters away to her mother about "how 'sprised papa will be to find that his little girl can knit like a grown-up woman," while Harry spreads out on the hearth a goodly store of shellbarks that he has gathered and is keeping for his share of the 'sprise.

"What if he shouldn't come?" asks Harry, suddenly.

"Oh, he'll come! Papa never stays away on Christmas," says Kitty, looking up into her mother's face for an echo to her words. Instead she sees something very like tears in her mother's eyes.

"Oh, mamma, don't you think he'll come?"

"He will come if he possibly can," says Mrs. Tracy; "and if he cannot, we will keep Christmas whenever dear papa does come home."

"It won't be half so nice," said Kitty, "nothing's so nice as REALLY Christmas, and how's Kriss Kringle going to know about it if we change the day?"

"We'll let him come just the same, and if he brings anything for papa we can put it away for him."

This plan, still, seemed a poor one to Miss Kitty, who went to her bed in a sober mood that night, and was heard telling her dear dollie, Martha Washington, that "wars were mis'able, and that when she married she should have a man who kept a candy-shop for a husband, and not a soldier—no, Martha, not even if he's as nice as papa!" As Martha made no objection to this little arrangement, being an obedient child, they were both soon fast asleep. The days of that cold winter of 1776 wore on; so cold it was that the sufferings of the soldiers were great, their bleeding feet often leaving marks on the pure white snow over which they marched. As Christmas drew near there was a feeling among the patriots that some blow was about to be struck; but what it was, and from whence they knew not; and, better than all, the British had no idea that any strong blow could come from Washington's army, weak and out of heart, as they thought, after being chased through Jersey by Cornwallis.

Mrs. Tracy looked anxiously each day for news of the husband and father only a few miles away, yet so separated by the river and the enemy's troops that they seemed like a hundred.

Christmas Eve came, but brought with it few rejoicings. The hearts of the people were too sad to be taken up with merrymaking, although the Hessian soldiers in the town, good-natured Germans, who only fought the Americans because they were paid for it, gave themselves up to the feasting and revelry.

"Shall we hang up our stockings?" asked Kitty, in rather a doleful voice.

"Yes," said her mother, "Santa Claus won't forget you, I am sure, although he has been kept pretty busy looking after the soldiers this winter."

"Which side is he on?" asked Harry.

"The right side, of course," said Mrs. Tracy, which was the most sensible answer she could possibly have given. So:

"The stockings were hung by the chimney with care, In hopes that St. Nicholas soon would be there."

Two little rosy faces lay fast asleep upon the pillow when the good old soul came dashing over the roof about one o'clock, and after filling each stocking with red apples, and leaving a cornucopia of sugar-plums for each child, he turned for a moment to look at the sleeping faces, for St. Nicholas has a tender spot in his great big heart for a soldier's children. Then, remembering many other small folks waiting for him all over the land, he sprang up the chimney and was away in a trice.

Santa Claus, in the form of Mrs. Tracy's farmer brother, brought her a splendid turkey; but because the Hessians were uncommonly fond of turkey, it came hidden under a load of wood. Harry was very fond of turkey, too, as well as of all other good things; but when his mother said, "It's such a fine bird, it seems too bad to eat it without father," Harry cried out, "Yes, keep it for papa!" and Kitty, joining in the chorus, the vote was unanimous, and the turkey was hung away to await the return of the good soldier, although it seemed strange, as Kitty told Martha Washington, "to have no papa and no turkey on Christmas Day."

The day passed and night came, cold with a steady fall of rain and sleet. Kitty prayed that her "dear papa might not be out in the storm, and that he might come home and wear his beautiful blue stockings"; "And eat his turkey," said Harry's sleepy voice; after which they were soon in the land of dreams. Toward morning the good people in Bordentown were suddenly aroused by firing in the distance, which became more and more distinct as the day wore on. There was great excitement in the town; men and women gathered together in little groups in the streets to wonder what it was all about, and neighbours came dropping into Mrs. Tracy's parlour, all day long, one after the other, to say what they thought of the firing. In the evening there came a body of Hessians flying into the town, to say that General Washington had surprised the British at Trenton, early that morning, and completely routed them, which so frightened the Hessians in Bordentown that they left without the slightest ceremony.

It was a joyful hour to the good town people when the red-jackets turned their backs on them, thinking every moment that the patriot army would be after them. Indeed, it seemed as if wonders would never cease that day, for while rejoicings were still loud, over the departure of the enemy, there came a knock at Mrs. Tracy's door, and while she was wondering whether she dared open it, it was pushed ajar, and a tall soldier entered. What a scream of delight greeted that soldier, and how Kitty and Harry danced about him and clung to his knees, while Mrs. Tracy drew him toward the warm blaze, and helped him off with his damp cloak!

Cold and tired Captain Tracy was, after a night's march in the streets and a day's fighting; but he was not too weary to smile at the dear faces around him, or to pat Kitty's head when she brought his warm stockings and would put them on the tired feet, herself.

Suddenly there was a sharp, quick bark outside the door. "What's that?" cried Harry.

"Oh, I forgot. Open the door. Here, Fido, Fido!"

Into the room there sprang a beautiful little King Charles spaniel, white, with tan spots, and ears of the longest, softest, and silkiest.

"What a little dear!" exclaimed Kitty; "where did it come from?"

"From the battle of Trenton," said her father. "His poor master was shot. After the red-coats had turned their backs, and I was hurrying along one of the streets where the fight had been the fiercest, I heard a low groan, and, turning, saw a British officer lying among a number of slain. I raised his head; he begged for some water, which I brought him, and bending down my ear I heard him whisper, 'Dying—last battle—say a prayer.' He tried to follow me in the words of a prayer, and then, taking my hand, laid it on something soft and warm, nestling close up to his breast—it was this little dog. The gentleman—for he was a real gentleman—gasped out, 'Take care of my poor Fido; good-night,' and was gone. It was as much as I could do to get the little creature away from his dead master; he clung to him as if he loved him better than life. You'll take care of him, won't you, children? I brought him home to you, for a Christmas present."

"Pretty little Fido," said Kitty, taking the soft, curly creature in her arms; "I think it's the best present in the world, and to-morrow is to be real Christmas, because you are home, papa."

"And we'll eat the turkey," said Harry, "and shellbarks, lots of them, that I saved for you. What a good time we'll have! And oh, papa, don't go to war any more, but stay at home, with mother and Kitty and Fido and me."

"What would become of our country if we should all do that, my little man? It was a good day's work that we did this Christmas, getting the army all across the river so quickly and quietly that we surprised the enemy, and gained a victory, with the loss of few men."

Thus it was that some of the good people of 1776 spent their Christmas, that their children and grandchildren might spend many of them as citizens of a free nation.

LITTLE PICCOLA

Nora Smith

"Story-telling is a real strengthening spirit-bath."—Froebel.

Piccola lived in Italy, where the oranges grow, and where all the year the sun shines warm and bright. I suppose you think Piccola a very strange name for a little girl; but in her country it was not strange at all, and her mother thought it the sweetest name a little girl ever had.

Piccola had no kind father, no big brother or sister, and no sweet baby to play with and love. She and her mother lived all alone in an old stone house that looked on a dark, narrow street. They were very poor, and the mother was away from home almost every day, washing clothes and scrubbing floors, and working hard to earn money for her little girl and herself. So you see Piccola was alone a great deal of the time; and if she had not been a very happy, contented little child, I hardly know what she would have done. She had no playthings except a heap of stones in the back yard that she used for building houses and a very old, very ragged doll that her mother had found in the street one day.

But there was a small round hole in the stone wall at the back of her yard, and her greatest pleasure was to look through that into her neighbor's garden. When she stood on a stone, and put her eyes close to the hole, she could see the green grass in the garden, and smell the sweet flowers, and even hear the water splashing into the fountain. She had never seen anyone walking in the garden, for it belonged to an old gentleman who did not care about grass and flowers.

One day in the autumn her mother told her that the old gentleman had gone away, and had rented his house to a family of little American children, who had come with their sick mother to spend the winter in Italy. After this, Piccola was never lonely, for all day long the children ran and played and danced and sang in the garden. It was several weeks before they saw her at all, and I am not sure they ever would have done so but one day the kitten ran away, and in chasing her they came close to the wall and saw Piccola's black eyes looking through the hole in the stones. They were a little frightened at first, and did not speak to her; but the next day she was there again, and Rose, the oldest girl, went up to the wall and talked to her a little while. When the children found that she had no one to play with and was very lonely, they talked to her every day, and often brought her fruits and candies, and passed them through the hole in the wall.

One day they even pushed the kitten through; but the hole was hardly large enough for her, and she mewed and scratched and was very much frightened. After that the little boy said he would ask his father if the hole might not be made larger, and then Piccola could come in and play with them. The father had found out that Piccola's mother was a good woman, and that the little girl herself was sweet and kind, so that he was very glad to have some of the stones broken away and an opening made for Piccola to come in.

How excited she was, and how glad the children were when she first stepped into the garden! She wore her best dress, a long, bright-colored woolen skirt and a white waist. Round her neck was a string of beads, and on her feet were little wooden shoes. It would seem very strange to us—would it not?—to wear wooden shoes; but Piccola and her mother had never worn anything else, and never had any money to buy stockings. Piccola almost always ran about barefooted, like the kittens and the chickens and the little ducks. What a good time they had that day, and how glad Piccola's mother was that her little girl could have such a pleasant, safe place to play in, while she was away at work!

By and by December came, and the little Americans began to talk about Christmas. One day, when Piccola's curly head and bright eyes came peeping through the hole in the wall, and they ran to her and helped her in; and as they did so, they all asked her at once what she thought she would have for a Christmas present. "A Christmas present!" said Piccola. "Why, what is that?"

All the children looked surprised at this, and Rose said, rather gravely, "Dear Piccola, don't you know what Christmas is?"

Oh, yes, Piccola knew it was the happy day when the baby Christ was born, and she had been to church on that day and heard the beautiful singing, and had seen the picture of the Babe lying in the manger, with cattle and sheep sleeping round about. Oh, yes, she knew all that very well, but what was a Christmas present?

Then the children began to laugh and to answer her all together. There was such a clatter of tongues that she could hear only a few of the words now and then, such as "chimney," "Santa Claus," "stockings," "reindeer," "Christmas Eve," "candies and toys." Piccola put her hands over her ears and said, "Oh, I can't understand one word. You tell me, Rose." Then Rose told her all about jolly Santa Claus, with his red cheeks and white beard and fur coat, and about his reindeer and sleigh full of toys. "Every Christmas Eve," said Rose, "he comes down the chimney, and fills the stockings of all the good children; so, Piccola, you hang up your stocking, and who knows what a beautiful Christmas present you will find when morning comes!" Of course Piccola thought this was a delightful plan, and was very pleased to hear about it. Then all the children told her of every Christmas Eve they could remember, and of the presents they had had; so that she went home thinking of nothing but dolls and hoops and balls and ribbons and marbles and wagons and kites.

She told her mother about Santa Claus, and her mother seemed to think that perhaps he did not know there was any little girl in that house, and very likely he would not come at all. But Piccola felt very sure Santa Claus would remember her, for her little friends had promised to send a letter up the chimney to remind him.

Christmas Eve came at last. Piccola's mother hurried home from her work; they had their little supper of soup and bread, and soon it was bedtime,—time to get ready for Santa Claus. But oh! Piccola remembered then for the first time that the children had told her she must hang up her stocking, and she hadn't any, and neither had her mother.

How sad, how sad it was! Now Santa Claus would come, and perhaps be angry because he couldn't find any place to put the present.

The poor little girl stood by the fireplace, and the big tears began to run down her cheeks. Just then her mother called to her, "Hurry, Piccola; come to bed." What should she do? But she stopped crying, and tried to think; and in a moment she remembered her wooden shoes, and ran off to get one of them. She put it close to the chimney, and said to herself, "Surely Santa

Claus will know what it's there for. He will know I haven't any stockings, so I gave him the shoe instead."

Then she went off happily to her bed, and was asleep almost as soon as she had nestled close to her mother's side.

The sun had only just begun to shine, next morning, when Piccola awoke. With one jump she was out on the floor and running toward the chimney. The wooden shoe was lying where she had left it, but you could never, never guess what was in it.

Piccola had not meant to wake her mother, but this surprise was more than any little girl could bear and yet be quiet; so she danced to the bed with the shoe in her hand, calling, "Mother, mother! look, look! see the present Santa Claus brought me!"

Her mother raised her head and looked into the shoe. "Why, Piccola," she said, "a little chimney swallow nestling in your shoe? What a good Santa Claus to bring you a bird!"

"Good Santa Claus, dear Santa Claus!" cried Piccola; and she kissed her mother and kissed the bird and kissed the shoe, and even threw kisses up the chimney, she was so happy.

When the birdling was taken out of the shoe, they found that he did not try to fly, only to hop about the room; and as they looked closer, they could see that one of his wings was hurt a little. But the mother bound it up carefully, so that it did not seem to pain him, and he was so gentle that he took a drink of water from a cup, and even ate crumbs and seeds out of Piccola's hands. She was a proud little girl when she took her Christmas present to show the children in the garden. They had had a great many gifts,—dolls that could say "mamma," bright picture books, trains of cars, toy pianos; but not one of their playthings was alive, like

Piccola's birdling. They were as pleased as she, and Rose hunted about the house until she found a large wicker cage that belonged to a blackbird she once had. She gave the cage to Piccola, and the swallow seemed to make himself quite at home in it at once, and sat on the perch winking his bright eyes at the children. Rose had saved a bag of candies for Piccola, and when she went home at last, with the cage and her dear swallow safely inside it, I am sure there was not a happier little girl in the whole country of Italy.

THE LEGEND OF BABOUSCKA (Adapted)

Carolyn S. Bailey

It was the night the dear Christ-Child came to Bethlehem. In a country far away from Him, an old, old woman named Babouscka sat in her snug little house by her warm fire. The wind was drifting the snow outside and howling down the chimney, but it only made Babouscka's fire burn more brightly.

"How glad I am that I may stay indoors," said Babouscka, holding her hands out to the bright blaze.

But suddenly she heard a loud rap at her door. She opened it and her candle shone on three old men standing outside in the snow. Their beards were as white as the snow, and so long that they reached the ground. Their eyes shone kindly in the light of Babouscka's candle, and their arms were full of precious things—boxes of jewels, and sweet-smelling oils, and ointments.

"We have travelled far, Babouscka," they said, "and we stop to tell you of the Baby Prince born this night in Bethlehem. He comes to rule the world and teach all men to be loving and true. We carry Him gifts. Come with us, Babouscka."

But Babouscka looked at the drifting snow, and then inside at her cozy room and the crackling fire. "It is too late for me to go with you, good sirs," she said, "the weather is too cold." She went inside again and shut the door, and the old men journeyed on to Bethlehem without her. But as Babouscka sat by her fire, rocking, she began to think about the Little Christ-Child, for she loved all babies.

"To-morrow I will go to find Him," she said; "to-morrow, when it is light, and I will carry Him some toys."

So when it was morning Babouscka put on her long cloak and took her staff, and filled her basket with the pretty things a baby would like—gold balls, and wooden toys, and strings of silver cobwebs—and she set out to find the Christ-Child.

But, oh, Babouscka had forgotten to ask the three old men the road to Bethlehem, and they travelled so far through the night that she could not overtake them. Up and down the road she hurried, through woods and fields and towns, saying to whomsoever she met: "I go to find the Christ-Child. Where does He lie? I bring some pretty toys for His sake."

But no one could tell her the way to go, and they all said: "Farther on, Babouscka, farther on." So she travelled on and on and on for years and years—but she never found the little Christ-Child.

They say that old Babouscka is travelling still, looking for Him. When it comes Christmas Eve, and the children are lying fast asleep, Babouscka comes softly through the snowy fields and towns, wrapped in her long cloak and carrying her basket on her arm. With her staff she raps gently at the doors and goes inside and holds her candle close to the little children's faces.

"Is He here?" she asks. "Is the little Christ-Child here?" And then she turns sorrowfully away again, crying: "Farther on, farther on!" But before she leaves she takes a toy from her basket and lays it beside the pillow for a Christmas gift. "For His sake," she says softly, and then hurries on through the years and forever in search of the little Christ-Child.

LITTLE GIRL'S CHRISTMAS

Winnifred E. Lincoln

It was Christmas Eve, and Little Girl had just hung up her stocking by the fireplace—right where it would be all ready for Santa when he slipped down the chimney. She knew he was coming, because—well, because it was Christmas Eve, and because he always had come to leave gifts for her on all the other Christmas Eves that she could remember, and because she had seen his pictures everywhere down town that afternoon when she was out with Mother.

Still, she wasn't JUST satisfied. 'Way down in her heart she was a little uncertain—you see, when you have never really and truly seen a person with your very own eyes, it's hard to feel as if you exactly believed in him—even though that person always has left beautiful gifts for you every time he has come.

"Oh, he'll come," said Little Girl; "I just know he will be here before morning, but somehow I wish—"

"Well, what do you wish?" said a Tiny Voice close by her—so close that Little Girl fairly jumped when she heard it.

"Why, I wish I could SEE Santa myself. I'd just like to go and see his house and his workshop, and ride in his sleigh, and know Mrs. Santa—'twould be such fun, and then I'd KNOW for sure."

"Why don't you go, then?" said Tiny Voice. "It's easy enough. Just try on these Shoes, and take this Light in your hand, and you'll find your way all right."

So Little Girl looked down on the hearth, and there were two cunning little Shoes side by side, and a little Spark of a Light close to them—just as if they were all made out of one of the glowing coals of the wood-fire. Such cunning Shoes as they were—Little Girl could hardly wait to pull off her slippers and try them on. They looked as if they were too small, but they weren't—they fitted exactly right, and just as Little Girl had put them both on and had taken the Light in her hand, along came a little Breath of Wind, and away she went up the chimney, along with ever so many other little Sparks, past the Soot Fairies, and out into the Open Air, where Jack Frost and the Star Beams were all busy at work making the world look pretty for Christmas.

Away went Little Girl—Two Shoes, Bright Light, and all—higher and higher, until she looked like a wee bit of a star up in the sky. It was the funniest thing, but she seemed to know the way perfectly, and didn't have to stop to make inquiries anywhere. You see it was a straight road all the way, and when one doesn't have to think about turning to the right or the left, it makes things very much easier. Pretty soon Little Girl noticed that there was a bright light all around her—oh, a very bright light—and right away something down in her heart began to make her feel very happy indeed. She didn't know that the Christmas spirits and little Christmas fairies were all around her and even right inside her, because she couldn't see a single one of them, even though her eyes were very bright and could usually see a great deal.

But that was just it, and Little Girl felt as if she wanted to laugh and sing and be glad. It made her remember the Sick Boy who lived next door, and she said to herself that she would carry him one of her prettiest picture-books in the morning, so that he could have something to make him happy all day. By and by, when the bright light all around her had grown very, very much brighter, Little Girl saw a path right in front of her, all straight and trim, leading up a hill to a big, big house with ever and ever so many windows in it. When she had gone just a bit nearer, she saw candles in every window, red and green and yellow ones, and every one burning brightly, so Little Girl knew right away that these were Christmas candles to light her on her journey, and make the way dear for her, and something told her that this was Santa's house, and that pretty soon she would perhaps see Santa himself.

Just as she neared the steps and before she could possibly have had time to ring the bell, the door opened—opened of itself as wide as could be—and there stood—not Santa himself—don't think it—but a funny Little Man with slender little legs and a roly-poly stomach which shook every now and then when he laughed. You would have known right away, just as Little Girl knew, that he was a very happy little man, and you would have guessed right away, too, that the reason he was so roly-poly was because he laughed and chuckled and smiled all the time—for it's only sour, cross folks who are thin and skimpy. Quick as a wink, he pulled off his little peaked red cap, smiled the broadest kind of a smile, and said, "Merry Christmas! Merry Christmas! Come in! Come in!"

So in went Little Girl, holding fast to Little Man's hand, and when she was really inside there was the jolliest, reddest fire all glowing and snapping, and there were Little Man and all his brothers and sisters, who said their names were "Merry Christmas," and "Good Cheer," and ever so many other jolly-sounding things, and there were such a lot of them that Little Girl just knew she never could count them, no matter how long she tried.

All around her were bundles and boxes and piles of toys and games, and Little Girl knew that these were all ready and waiting to be loaded into Santa's big sleigh for his reindeer to whirl them away over cloudtops and snowdrifts to the little people down below who had left their stockings all ready for him. Pretty soon all the little Good Cheer Brothers began to hurry and bustle and carry out the bundles as fast as they could to the steps where Little Girl could hear the jingling bells and the stamping of hoofs. So Little Girl picked up some bundles and skipped along too, for she wanted to help a bit herself—it's no fun whatever at Christmas unless you can help, you know—and there in the yard stood the BIGGEST sleigh that Little Girl had ever seen, and the reindeer were all stamping and prancing and jingling the bells on their harnesses, because they were so eager to be on their way to the Earth once more.

She could hardly wait for Santa to come, and just as she had begun to wonder where he was, the door opened again and out came a whole forest of Christmas trees, at least it looked just as if a whole forest had started out for a walk somewhere, but a second glance showed Little Girl that there were thousands of Christmas sprites, and that each one carried a tree or a big Christmas wreath on his back. Behind them all, she could hear some one laughing loudly, and talking in a big, jovial voice that sounded as if he were good friends with the whole world.

And straightway she knew that Santa himself was coming. Little Girl's heart went pit-a-pat for a minute while she wondered if Santa would notice her, but she didn't have to wonder long, for he spied her at once and said:

"Bless my soul! who's this? and where did you come from?"

Little Girl thought perhaps she might be afraid to answer him, but she wasn't one bit afraid. You see he had such a kind little twinkle in his eyes that she felt happy right away as she replied, "Oh, I'm Little Girl, and I wanted so much to see Santa that I just came, and here I am!"

"Ho, ho, ho, ho, ho!" laughed Santa, "and here you are! Wanted to see Santa, did you, and so you came! Now that's very nice, and it's too bad I'm in such a hurry, for we should like nothing better than to show you about and give you a real good time. But you see it is quarter of twelve now, and I must be on my way at once, else I'll never reach that first chimney-top by midnight. I'd call Mrs. Santa and ask her to get you some supper, but she is busy finishing dolls' clothes which must be done before morning, and I guess we'd better not bother her. Is there anything that you would like, Little Girl?" and good old Santa put his big warm hand on Little Girl's curls and she felt its warmth and kindness clear down to her very heart. You see, my dears, that even though Santa was in such a great hurry, he wasn't too busy to stop and make some one happy for a minute, even if it was some one no bigger than Little Girl.

So she smiled back into Santa's face and said: "Oh, Santa, if I could ONLY ride down to Earth with you behind those splendid reindeer! I'd love to go; won't you PLEASE take me? I'm so small that I won't take up much room on the seat, and I'll keep very still and not bother one bit!"

Then Santa laughed, SUCH a laugh, big and loud and rollicking, and he said, "Wants a ride, does she? Well, well, shall we take her, Little Elves? Shall we take her, Little Fairies? Shall we take her, Good Reindeer?"

And all the Little Elves hopped and skipped and brought Little Girl a sprig of holly; and all the Little Fairies bowed and smiled and brought her a bit of mistletoe; and all the Good Reindeer jingled their bells loudly, which meant, "Oh, yes! let's take her! She's a good Little Girl! Let her ride!" And before Little Girl could even think, she found herself all tucked up in the big fur robes beside Santa, and away they went, right out into the air, over the clouds, through the Milky Way, and right under the very handle of the Big Dipper, on, on, toward the Earthland, whose lights Little Girl began to see twinkling away down below her. Presently she felt the runners scrape upon something, and she knew they must be on some one's roof, and that Santa would slip down some one's chimney in a minute.

How she wanted to go, too! You see if you had never been down a chimney and seen Santa fill up the stockings, you would want to go quite as much as Little Girl did, now, wouldn't you? So, just as Little Girl was wishing as hard as ever she could wish, she heard a Tiny Voice say, "Hold tight to his arm! Hold tight to his arm!" So she held Santa's arm tight and close, and he shouldered his pack, never thinking that it was heavier than usual, and with a bound and a slide, there they were, Santa, Little Girl, pack and all, right in the middle of a room where there was a fireplace and stockings all hung up for Santa to fill.

Just then Santa noticed Little Girl. He had forgotten all about her for a minute, and he was very much surprised to find that she had come, too. "Bless my soul!" he said, "where did you come from, Little Girl? and how in the world can we both get back up that chimney again? It's easy enough to slide down, but it's quite another matter to climb up again!" and Santa looked real worried. But Little Girl was beginning to feel very tired by this time, for she had had a very exciting evening, so she said, "Oh, never mind me, Santa. I've had such a good time, and I'd just as soon stay here a while as not. I believe I'll curl up on his hearth-rug a few minutes and have a little nap, for it looks as warm and cozy as our own hearth-rug at home, and—why, it is our own hearth and it's my own nursery, for there is Teddy Bear in his chair where I leave him every night, and there's Bunny Cat curled up on his cushion in the corner."

And Little Girl turned to thank Santa and say goodbye to him, but either he had gone very quickly, or else she had fallen asleep very quickly—she never could tell which—for the next thing she knew, Daddy was holding her in his arms and was saying, "What is my Little Girl doing here? She must go to bed, for it's Christmas Eve, and old Santa won't come if he thinks there are any little folks about."

But Little Girl knew better than that, and when she began to tell him all about it, and how the Christmas fairies had welcomed her, and how Santa had given her such a fine ride, Daddy laughed and laughed, and said, "You've been dreaming, Little Girl, you've been dreaming."

But Little Girl knew better than that, too, for there on the hearth was the little Black Coal, which had given her Two Shoes and Bright Light, and tight in her hand she held a holly berry which one of the Christmas Sprites had placed there. More than all that, there she was on the hearth-rug herself, just as Santa had left her, and that was the best proof of all.

The trouble was, Daddy himself had never been a Little Girl, so he couldn't tell anything about it, but we know she hadn't been dreaming, now, don't we, my dears?

THE STAR

Florence M. Kingsley

Once upon a time in a country far away from here, there lived a little girl named Ruth. Ruth's home was not at all like our houses, for she lived in a little tower on top of the great stone wall that surrounded the town of Bethlehem. Ruth's father was the hotel-keeper—the Bible says the "inn keeper." This inn was not at all like our hotels, either. There was a great open yard, which was called the courtyard. All about this yard were little rooms and each traveler who came to the hotel rented one. The inn stood near the great stone wall of the city, so that as Ruth stood, one night, looking out of the tower window, she looked directly into the courtyard. It was truly a strange sight that met her eyes. So many people were coming to the inn, for the King had made a law that every man should come back to the city where his father used to live to be counted and to pay his taxes. Some of the people came on the backs of camels, with great rolls of bedding and their dishes for cooking upon the back of the beast. Some of them came on little donkeys, and on their backs too were the bedding and the dishes. Some of the people came walking— slowly; they were so tired. Many miles some of them had come. As Ruth looked down into the courtyard, she saw the camels being led to their places by their masters, she heard the snap of the whips, she saw the sparks shoot up from the fires that were kindled in the courtyard, where each per[Pg 160]son was preparing his own supper; she heard the cries of the tired, hungry little children.

Presently her mother, who was cooking supper, came over to the window and said, "Ruthie, thou shalt hide in the house until all those people are gone. Dost thou understand?"

"Yes, my mother," said the child, and she left the window to follow her mother back to the stove, limping painfully, for little Ruth was a cripple. Her mother stooped suddenly and caught the child in her arms.

"My poor little lamb. It was a mule's kick, just six years ago, that hurt your poor back and made you lame."

"Never mind, my mother. My back does not ache today, and lately when the light of the strange new star has shone down upon my bed my back has felt so much stronger and I have felt so happy, as though I could climb upon the rays of the star and up, up into the sky and above the stars!"

Her mother shook her head sadly. "Thou art not likely to climb much, now or ever, but come, the supper is ready; let us go to find your father. I wonder what keeps him."

They found the father standing at the gate of the courtyard, talking to a man and woman who had just arrived. The man was tall, with a long beard, and he led by a rope a snow white mule, on which sat the drooping figure of the woman. As Ruth and her mother came near, they heard the father say, "But I tell thee that there is no more room in the inn. Hast thou no friends where thou canst go to spend the night?" The man shook his head. "No, none," he answered. "I care not for myself, but my poor wife." Little Ruth pulled at her mother's [Pg 161]dress. "Mother, the oxen sleep out under the stars these warm nights and the straw in the caves is clean and warm; I have made a bed there for my little lamb."

Ruth's mother bowed before the tall man. "Thou didst hear the child. It is as she says—the straw is clean and warm." The tall man bowed his head. "We shall be very glad to stay," and he helped the sweet-faced woman down from the donkey's back and led her away to the cave stable, while the little Ruth and her mother hurried up the stairs that they might send a bowl of porridge to the sweet-faced woman, and a sup of new milk, as well.

That night when little Ruth lay down in her bed, the rays of the beautiful new star shone through the window more brightly than before. They seemed to soothe the tired aching shoulders. She fell asleep and dreamed that the beautiful, bright star burst and out of it came countless angels, who sang in the night:

"Glory to God in the highest, peace on earth, good will to men." And then it was morning and her mother was bending over her and saying, "Awake, awake, little Ruth. Mother has something to tell thee." Then as the eyes opened slowly—"The angels came in the night, little one, and left a Baby to lay beside your little white lamb in the manger."

That afternoon, Ruth went with her mother to the fountain. The mother turned aside to talk to the other women of the town about the strange things heard and seen the night before, but Ruth went on and sat down by the edge of the fountain. The child, was not frightened, [Pg 162]for strangers came often to the well, but never had she seen men who looked like the three who now came towards her. The first one, a tall man with a long white beard, came close to Ruth and said, "Canst tell us, child, where is born he that is called the King of the Jews?"

"I know of no king," she answered, "but last night while the star was shining, the angels brought a baby to lie beside my white lamb in the manger." The stranger bowed his head. "That must be he. Wilt thou show us the way to Him, my child?" So Ruth ran and her mother led the three men to the cave and "when they saw the Child, they rejoiced with exceeding great joy, and opening their gifts, they presented unto Him gold, and frankincense and myrrh," with wonderful jewels, so that Ruth's mother's eyes shone with wonder, but little Ruth saw only the Baby, which lay asleep on its mother's breast.

"If only I might hold Him in my arms," she thought, but was afraid to ask.

After a few days, the strangers left Bethlehem, all but the three—the man, whose name was Joseph, and Mary, his wife, and the Baby. Then, as of old, little Ruth played about the courtyard and the white lamb frolicked at her side. Often she dropped to her knees to press the little woolly white head against her breast, while she murmured: "My little lamb, my very, very own. I love you, lambie," and then together they would steal over to the entrance of the cave to peep in at the Baby, and always she thought, "If I only might touch his hand," but was afraid to ask. One night as she lay in her bed, she thought to herself: "Oh, I wish I had a [Pg 163]beautiful gift for him, such as the wise men brought, but I have nothing at all to offer and I love him so much." Just then the light of the star, which was nightly fading, fell across the foot of the bed and shone full upon the white lamb which lay asleep at her feet—and then she thought of something. The next morning she arose with her face shining with joy. She dressed carefully and with the white lamb held close to her breast, went slowly and painfully down the stairway and over to the door of the cave. "I have come," she said, "to worship Him, and I have brought Him—my white lamb." The mother smiled at the lame child, then she lifted the Baby from her breast and placed Him in the arms of the little maid who knelt at her feet.

A few days after, an angel came to the father, Joseph, and told him to take the Baby and hurry to the land of Egypt, for the wicked King wanted to do it harm, and so these three—the father, mother and Baby—went by night to the far country of Egypt. And the star grew dimmer and dimmer and passed away forever from the skies over Bethlehem, but little Ruth grew straight and strong and beautiful as the almond trees in the orchard, and all the people who saw her were amazed, for Ruth was once a cripple.

"It was the light of the strange star," her mother said, but little Ruth knew it was the touch of the blessed Christ-Child, who was once folded against her heart.

WHY THE CHIMES RANG

Raymond McAlden

There was once in a faraway country where few people have ever travelled, a wonderful church. It stood on a high hill in the midst of a great city; and every Sunday, as well as on sacred days like Christmas, thousands of people climbed the hill to its great archways, looking like lines of ants all moving in the same direction.

When you came to the building itself, you found stone columns and dark passages, and a grand entrance leading to the main room of the church. This room was so long that one standing at the doorway could scarcely see to the other end, where the choir stood by the marble altar. In the farthest corner was the organ; and this organ was so loud, that sometimes when it played, the people for miles around would close their shutters and prepare for a great thunderstorm. Altogether, no such church as this was ever seen before, especially when it was lighted up for some festival, and crowded with people, young and old. But the strangest thing about the whole building was the wonderful chime of bells.

At one corner of the church was a great gray tower, with ivy growing over it as far up as one could see. I say as far as one could see, because the tower was quite great enough to fit the great church, and it rose so far into the sky that it was only in very fair weather that any one claimed to be able to see the top. Even then one could not be certain that it was in sight. Up, and up, and up climbed the stones and the ivy; and as the men who built the church had been dead for hundreds of years, every one had forgotten how high the tower was supposed to be.

Now all the people knew that at the top of the tower was a chime of Christmas bells. They had hung there ever since the church had been built, and were the most beautiful bells in the world. Some thought it was because a great musician had cast them and arranged them in their place; others said it was because of the great height, which reached up where the air was clearest and purest; however that might be no one who had ever heard the chimes denied that they were the sweetest in the world. Some described them as sounding like angels far up in the sky; others as sounding like strange winds singing through the trees.

But the fact was that no one had heard them for years and years. There was an old man living not far from the church who said that his mother had spoken of hearing them when she was a little girl, and he was the only one who was sure of as much as that. They were Christmas chimes, you see, and were not meant to be played by men or on common days. It was the custom on Christmas Eve for all the people to bring to the church their offerings to the Christ-Child; and when the greatest and best offering was laid on the altar there used to come sounding through the music of the choir the Christmas chimes far up in the tower. Some said that the wind rang them, and others, that they were so high that the angels could set them swinging. But for many long years they had never been heard. It was said that people had been growing less careful of their gifts for the Christ-Child, and that no offering was brought great enough to deserve the music of the chimes.

Every Christmas Eve the rich people still crowded to the altar, each one trying to bring some better gift than any other, without giving anything that he wanted for himself, and the church was crowded with those who thought that perhaps the wonderful bells might be heard again. But although the service was splendid, and the offerings plenty, only the roar of the wind could be heard, far up in the stone tower.

Now, a number of miles from the city, in a little country village, where nothing could be seen of the great church but glimpses of the tower when the weather was fine, lived a boy named Pedro, and his little brother. They knew very little about the Christmas chimes, but they had heard of the service in the church on Christmas Eve, and had a secret plan which they had often talked over when by themselves, to go to see the beautiful celebration.

"Nobody can guess, Little Brother," Pedro would say; "all the fine things there are to see and hear; and I have even heard it said that the Christ-Child sometimes comes down to bless the service. What if we could see Him?"

The day before Christmas was bitterly cold, with a few lonely snowflakes flying in the air, and a hard white crust on the ground. Sure enough Pedro and Little Brother were able to slip quietly away early in the afternoon; and although the walking was hard in the frosty air, before nightfall they had trudged so far, hand in hand, that they saw the lights of the big city just ahead of them. Indeed they were about to enter one of the great gates in the wall that surrounded it, when they saw something dark on the snow near their path, and stepped aside to look at it.

It was a poor woman, who had fallen just outside the city, too sick and tired to get in where she might have found shelter. The soft snow made of a drift a sort of pillow for her, and she would soon be so sound asleep, in the wintry air, that no one could ever waken her again. All this Pedro saw in a moment and he knelt down beside her and tried to rouse her, even tugging at her arm a little, as though he would have tried to carry her away. He turned her face toward him, so that he could rub some of the snow on it, and when he had looked at her silently a moment he stood up again, and said:

"It's no use, Little Brother. You will have to go on alone."

"Alone?" cried Little Brother. "And you not see the Christmas festival?"

"No," said Pedro, and he could not keep back a bit of a choking sound in his throat. "See this poor woman. Her face looks like the Madonna in the chapel window, and she will freeze to death if nobody cares for her. Every one has gone to the church now, but when you come back you can bring some one to help her. I will rub her to keep her from freezing, and perhaps get her to eat the bun that is left in my pocket."

"But I cannot bear to leave you, and go on alone," said Little Brother.

"Both of us need not miss the service," said Pedro, "and it had better be I than you. You can easily find your way to church; and you must see and hear everything twice, Little Brother—once for you and once for me. I am sure the Christ-Child must know how I should love to come with you and worship Him; and oh! if you get a chance, Little Brother, to slip up to the altar without getting in any one's way, take this little silver piece of mine, and lay it down for my offering, when no one is looking. Do not forget where you have left me, and forgive me for not going with you."

In this way he hurried Little Brother off to the city and winked hard to keep back the tears, as he heard the crunching footsteps sounding farther and farther away in the twilight. It was pretty hard to lose the music and splendour of the Christmas celebration that he had been planning for so long, and spend the time instead in that lonely place in the snow.

The great church was a wonderful place that night. Every one said that it had never looked so bright and beautiful before. When the organ played and the thousands of people sang, the walls shook with the sound, and little Pedro, away outside the city wall, felt the earth tremble around them.

At the close of the service came the procession with the offerings to be laid on the altar. Rich men and great men marched proudly up to lay down their gifts to the Christ-Child. Some brought wonderful jewels, some baskets of gold so heavy that they could scarcely carry them down the aisle. A great writer laid down a book that he had been making for years and years. And last of all walked the king of the country, hoping with all the rest to win for himself the chime of the Christmas bells. There went a great murmur through the church as the people saw the king take from his head the royal crown, all set with precious stones, and lay it gleaming on the altar, as his offering to the Holy Child. "Surely," every one said, "we shall hear the bells now, for nothing like this has ever happened before."

But still only the cold old wind was heard in the tower and the people shook their heads; and some of them said, as they had before, that they never really believed the story of the chimes, and doubted if they ever rang at all.

The procession was over, and the choir began the closing hymn. Suddenly the organist stopped playing; and every one looked at the old minister, who was standing by the altar, holding up his hand for silence. Not a sound could be heard from any one in the church, but as all the people strained their ears to listen, there came softly, but distinctly, swinging through the air, the sound of the chimes in the tower. So far away, and yet so clear the music seemed—so much sweeter were the notes than anything that had been heard before, rising and falling away up there in the sky, that the people in the church sat for a moment as still as though something held each of them by the shoulders. Then they all stood up together and stared straight at the altar, to see what great gift had awakened the long silent bells.

But all that the nearest of them saw was the childish figure of Little Brother, who had crept softly down the aisle when no one was looking, and had laid Pedro's little piece of silver on the altar.

Made in the USA
Monee, IL
01 December 2022